To Karen

HIS FIRST FAMILY

VICTORIA SUE

Victoria Sue x

Cover design: Jay Aheer

Editing: Miranda Vescio

CONTENTS

Every author likes to think they put a little of themselves in a book, but this was very personal to me. To all the moms, dads, alphas, and omegas who have had their babies in an ICU, I know what you are going through. I understand the helplessness when you can't be what you envisioned to your newborn. I understand the horror of leaving them there and having to go home. I understand the dread of visiting every day and terrified something will go wrong. I celebrate with every parent who managed to bring their little one home, but I especially stand with every parent who never got to do that.

This book is for you.

ONE

"YOU WANT ME TO *LEAVE*?" Lorne Austin stared at his alpha in complete bewilderment.

Stephen Carmichael had the grace to look uncomfortable and somewhat out of place standing in the small bedroom on the third floor which had been his for the past sixteen years.

"The twins are fifteen," the alpha continued as if he was likely to forget. "And, as such, you are no longer a mated omega. You're free to do whatever you like. To *go* wherever you like."

Lorne stared uncomprehendingly. He knew they were fifteen. Of course he did. He spent a long day putting together a huge party that was to start as soon as their elder brother Nicholas arrived from the city. He had just popped up to his room to get changed, hoping he would be included when the girls got to open their presents since he made them a gift. He had been stunned to find his alpha and mistress waiting for him.

"You have told us on numerous occasions you would never wish to go live at an omega retirement complex," Alpha Stephen said.

Because I want to stay here. This was his home. He would never want to leave. And Mistress had dropped so many hints over the years regarding his future. How their hands were tied when it came to omega contracts because they were the law, and as a top class attorney, she could hardly be seen to be doing anything illegal, but as soon as the girls were fifteen, things would be different. They had even hinted about extending the already huge house to build him his own suite. He was happy with his room, and even if they had never managed to remodel the heating to extend it to the third floor, he had always managed.

"I want you gone before Sophie and Suzanna open their presents to save any awkwardness. I'm sure you wouldn't be so selfish as to ruin their birthday—"

"I would *never*." The very thought horrified Lorne.

"Exactly." Alpha Stephen seemed pleased. "I knew you would understand." He glanced at his watch. "You had better hurry."

"You want me to leave *now*?" Lorne knew his normally trained softly spoken voice was getting louder by the frown on his mistress's face, but he didn't care. He just didn't understand what they meant. He was staying here. He had *always* thought he was staying here. All mated omegas' contracts ended when the last of their alpha's children reached fifteen. Of course, his contract had always been a little different in that his mistress was the one to actually get pregnant and have the children, but he had been waiting with open arms immediately after they were born, had fed them their first bottles, changed their first diapers, and been there every time they had woken during the night.

And he had loved every second. His only regret was never actually going through a birth, but as the mistress had pointed out, it was easier for her. Female bodies were naturally designed to have children. Male omegas had to be helped by science developed after the great wars had ended, and it would be inconvenient for the master and mistress to have to take him to the omega clinic to deliver.

"Lorne, please understand; we are in a difficult position." Elspeth Carmichael smiled, and Lorne shivered. He had always imagined her using that look to give a defendant a false sense of security before she annihilated them on the witness stand. "At fifteen, the girls don't need you anymore, and we were thinking of remodeling this floor to include an office suite for Nicholas. So, we have rented a place for you in a little community outside of Granley in the northern sector. It's quite rural. Lots of fresh air and exercise will be good for you, and we know how much you like animals. You could get a puppy."

A puppy? "But—"

"We have ordered you a cab. It will be here in ten minutes which will give you enough time to pack a small bag."

Lorne stared at his alpha. He couldn't believe— "But the party—"

"Is being fully catered," his mistress said.

"Ten minutes?" he squeaked out.

"Actually," his mistress glanced at her watch, "I believe the cab will be here by now." She nodded as if everything was agreed and turned, leaving the room.

Lorne looked at his alpha on the off chance he was having a nightmare and they really weren't expecting him to go, but he just made a small shooing movement with his fingers. He was dismissed.

In a complete and utter daze, Lorne looked around his room, taking in the small bed with the mattress you had to lie on in a certain way to avoid the spring that stuck up, the peeling wallpaper he had tried to stick down so many times, and the chilly air. It had snowed over Christmas—it was still snowing heavily—and he had been freezing, but too exhausted every night when he had fallen into bed to care about anything other than setting his alarm for a bare seven hours later.

He glanced down at his belly, almost as if he was going to see the bruises where he'd just been kicked, or at least, it felt like he'd just been kicked. Neither the alpha nor his mistress had ever laid a hand on him of course.

It must be a mistake. Sixteen years. Sixteen years from the day he had been collected from the omega development offices. His parents had always wanted rid of him, and even if he couldn't be legally mated until the next year when he would turn eighteen, his parents hadn't seemed to care. Alpha Stephen had just remarried after his wife and their omega had died in a car accident, leaving behind him and a twelve-year-old son, Nicholas. He had brought his new wife, and they chose Lorne.

And he had been so happy. Nicholas was such a prickly child. He had lost his mom and omega just when he needed them the most, but they quickly became good friends. Especially after Nicholas was given the enchiladas the new cook had been instructed to make. Nicholas's nut allergy was severe, but it was Lorne who had immediately administered the EpiPen when the mistress panicked as Nicholas struggled to breathe.

Lorne hadn't understood her reaction. The cook was fired even though she insisted she had never been warned of Nicholas's allergy. He'd always thought it odd the mistress would be so careless, and she usually never panicked over anything, even when the EpiPen wasn't in its usual spot in one of the kitchen drawers like usual. It was fortunate Lorne was so organized he had ordered some spare ones and stored them upstairs.

And he wouldn't even get to see Nicholas now.

"Here." Alpha Stephen held out an envelope. "Some cash to tide you over, but like I said, the room is paid for and the details are in there," he continued and stood awkwardly while Lorne threw his few outfits in a small case. It was the same case his mom and dad had dropped him off carrying all those years ago. There might be a few more clothes in there than the last time, but there were still no possessions. Omegas didn't own anything.

He quickly gathered up the small folder lying on his bedside table then gazed in bewilderment around the room. Not an inch of wall space was left that didn't contain a drawing either Nicholas, Suzanna, or Sophie had presented him with over the years. They hadn't been allowed to buy him actual gifts, and Lorne was glad. These meant more to him than anything. Even when he'd passed his thirtieth birthday, which signified the end to an omega's fertility, he hadn't grieved over not having his own family, because Nicholas, Suzanna, and Sophie filled that role.

"I'll send them on," Alpha Stephen said gruffly. Lorne nodded, picked up his small case, and followed the alpha downstairs. He didn't look at anything as he went down. He didn't glance at the nursery. He'd slept in there on a cot for over a year after the girls were born. The alpha himself had suggested it because his wife had an important job and it was essential she got a good night's sleep every night. Even when the night feedings stopped, he had still been there for chicken pox, runny noses, and fevers whenever he was needed. He kept his head firmly forward and just headed for the front door.

The alpha closed it behind him without saying a word.

JONATHAN PROPPED his feet up on another stool and watched the fire. It wasn't exactly the beach vacation he had planned, but it had been worth every cent of his wasted airfare to see Gabe and Bo happily married. He glanced out of the window. He was going to drive back to the omega clinic—even if he was still officially on vacation—to see if they needed a hand, but his BMW wasn't designed for snowy roads, and he doubted if he would be able to get anywhere under the current near blizzard conditions. He glanced at the clock above the bar. Seven p.m. and he was still waiting on his supper. The small pub wasn't used to paying guests, but he had no intention of staying with Gabe and Bo when they were essentially on their honeymoon, and the landlord had a few spare rooms he had hastily cleaned out. Last night another three people— stranded like him—had joined them, and the place was now full.

"I'm sorry. I just have absolutely no idea where I'm going to put you."

Jonathan turned his head. From his corner of the bar, he could see the entrance and the man who had just walked in. Henry, the landlord, looked apologetic. He couldn't see the man's face, but he took in the droop of his shoulders and the wet hair. His eyes traveled down, and he winced at the soaking wet pants and shoes. He looked like he'd hiked in the snow but was dressed for a day at the office.

The man said something, but he was so softly spoken Jonathan couldn't hear what he said.

"Obviously, you can wait in the bar," Henry continued. He looked him up and down. "I can see if any of the guests have spare clothes while we dry yours." Jonathan stood up. The man must be nearly six feet tall and very slim; Henry was five feet four on a good day, and his belly was proof of how much he enjoyed his own beer.

"Henry?" Jonathan started walking up to the bar. "I have—" And then he forgot what he was about to say as the man turned around and Jonathan was transfixed by the most unusual blue eyes he had ever seen in his entire life. They were almost violet.

Jonathan blinked and realized either the man or Henry had said something, but he had no clue what it had been. He stuck his hand out. "Jonathan Owens." He never introduced himself as *Dr.* Owens. Apart from it being pretentious, it could often lead to uncomfortable conversations where people expected him to diagnose them on the spot. Or they had the most unusual condition in the world they were sure Jonathan had never heard of.

Usually, most of them turned out to be things he wouldn't want to.

"L-Lorne Austin." A slim but very cold hand slid into his, and Jonathan, frowning and before he questioned it, covered the man's hand with his other as well. "You're freezing."

The blue eyes dimmed a little. "Little bit." And Jonathan took in the shiver the man was trying to suppress. He let go and looked at Henry. "I have some spare clothes. Mr. Austin can come with me." Jonathan further took in his cold and bedraggled state. "You need a hot bath. Henry?" He glanced at the landlord. "Please send supper upstairs." And giving neither of them a chance to answer, he steered the bewildered looking man—*Lorne*—to the stairs.

"Do you have a case?" He didn't seem to be carrying a bag.

"I did," Lorne said. "The clasp broke. I had to leave it wedged under a bush about one, maybe two, miles back."

Jonathan opened his mouth to ask a ton of questions, but now wasn't the time. He didn't like the pallor of the man's skin even if it did make his eyes even more stunning. He needed to get him warm, dry, and fed. Then they could talk. He opened the door to the room he had been given and turned back to see Lorne looking around seeming unsure of what to do.

He smiled encouragingly. "If you would like me to wait downstairs while you take a bath—"

"No," Lorne said hurriedly. "I would never dream...this is your room, and you are being very generous."

Jonathan nodded and walked into the small adjoining bathroom, turning on the faucet. Hot water immediately started filling the large tub. Henry had assured him their fires fed the water, so even if the electricity went out, they would still be warm. He walked back into the room and saw Lorne hadn't moved. "Go on," He nodded to the bathroom. "There's towels in there, and I'll get you some clothes... *Lorne*." He added his name a little louder because the man seemed in a daze, but he jolted slightly at Jonathan's firmer tone.

"Yes, Alpha," he mumbled, hurried to the bathroom, and closed the door behind him.

Alpha? Jonathan never enforced his alpha status. Half the nurses he worked with only ever said it in fun, and these days, even though it had originally been used as a term of respect, the alpha-holes who insisted on it were usually the least deserving of any. Maybe it was an automatic response to Jonathan giving instructions? Maybe Lorne was an omega? Probably, but none of that mattered in the current situation.

Jonathan went to the dresser and pulled out some shorts and a T-shirt. He added some socks to the pile. Then he stopped. He'd forgotten he had packed for a beach. Gabe had loaned him the sweatpants he was wearing, but he didn't have any others. He had his dress suit he'd worn to the wedding, and that was it. He'd originally planned to fly out and start his vacation a day later, but the snow had brought everything to a halt. Then he remembered the robe hanging on the bathroom door, but just as he was going to tell Lorne where it was, Henry's wife Molly arrived with their supper. Jonathan inhaled appreciatively as he took the tray.

"It's homemade chili, and the bread was baked this morning." Jonathan groaned. He was starving, and it smelled fantastic. Molly chuckled. "And Henry said to say the gentleman is welcome to push a few chairs together downstairs. I have some blankets, just no more couches."

"We'll manage," Jonathan assured her. Lorne could have his bed. He'd sleep on the floor. It might have been a long time since he had done that, but it would hardly kill him.

He went to the bathroom door and knocked. "I have some clothes here and supper just got delivered."

Silence.

Jonathan tried again. "Lorne? Are you okay?"

When his second question didn't illicit a reply, concern rippled down his spine, and without hesitation, he pushed open the door. Lorne was lying up to his neck in steaming water, and his eyes were closed. In fact, he looked asleep.

And *naked*. Obviously, considering he was submerged in water. But Jonathan got a view of nice defined muscles and smooth skin. And—*yeah*—he looked away. "Lorne?" he bent down and touched his shoulder. Lorne smiled and lazily cracked his eyes open. A second passed, then Lorne's eyes widened dramatically, and he jerked upright. "It's okay," soothed Jonathan. "I knocked, but you were asleep." He carried on talking as he backed farther away. "Supper's here." He nodded to the clothes on the stool. "That's all I have, but there's a robe behind the door." He yanked it down and added it to the pile of clothes then closed the door.

And took a breath. Lorne was gorgeous. He would guess them to be similar in age, but his smooth pale skin didn't look like it even needed a razor. And those eyes. And...he groaned. He couldn't unsee the smooth muscles or... He glanced down at himself, suddenly glad Gabe's sweats were a little larger than he normally wore.

He pulled a second chair over from the corner of the room toward the small desk he'd put the tray on and noted Henry had even poured a couple of beers and added them to the spread. He rubbed his hands just as the door opened.

Lorne stood wrapped in the robe, and Jonathan ran a critical eye over him. Still pale. "Come, sit. Molly said to leave your pants outside the bedroom door and she'd collect them with the tray. They'll be dry in the morning."

Lorne swallowed and glanced at the food as if it was going to eat *him*. Jonathan smiled and pulled a chair out. "I don't bite," he said jokingly then almost groaned at the image it put in his head. He'd been trying to forget the sight of Lorne in the bath.

"This is very kind of you, Alpha," Lorne murmured as he sat down.

"Jonathan, please. I don't go in for all that alpha status."

And for the first time, Lorne smiled. Jonathan just wasn't convinced it wasn't because Lorne thought the idea of not going all alpha on him was ridiculous. He would just have to prove it he guessed.

"Molly's a good cook, and Henry sent up some of his beer. He brews it himself." Jonathan sat, knowing he was babbling for some reason, and took a sip of his beer to keep his mouth occupied. He closed his eyes at *that* thought and tried to think of something else other than the delicious view he had gotten of Lorne. He opened his eyes because keeping them closed wasn't really helping.

"I've never had any beer," Lorne said shyly and took a sip. His eyes widened a little. "It tastes a little of blackberry."

Jonathan grinned. "Yep. I came here for the first time two days ago, but I have good friends who live near, so I plan on being a regular." Lorne's smile faded, and he glanced at his food. Jonathan wondered what he'd said to cause it. "I was at their wedding. I was actually supposed to be leaving straight after, but the weather got worse. Gabe wanted me to stay with them but that would be one too many for their honeymoon, so I said I would bunk here."

Lorne took a bite of chili then another sip of beer.

"You got stranded, huh?" Jonathan prompted when it didn't seem Lorne was going to volunteer anything.

"I'm just moving to the area," Lorne said. "But the cab refused to come off the highway because he said his car would get stuck, so I had to walk."

What? "You mean the Northern Expressway?" Jonathan asked. "But that's a good seven miles away."

Lorne smiled ruefully. "It felt like it."

"Where are you heading?"

Lorne took another sip of his beer and seemed surprised to see he was halfway down the glass. "From what the cabby said, I'm not that far away from where I'm renting. I'll check it out tomorrow." Jonathan wanted to ask where, but he managed to rein himself in. They ate in silence for a good few minutes. Lorne drained his beer, and Jonathan liked the pink that was beginning to color his cheeks.

Lorne stood and took his and Jonathan's empty plates and put them on the tray. "I'll take the dishes down with me." He picked up his folded pants from the floor and wrinkled his nose a little.

"Molly said just to leave them outside with the tray," Jonathan said, wondering what Lorne was doing.

He looked up, an embarrassed flush deepening the color on his face. "I can't go downstairs without pants."

Jonathan chuckled in understanding. "You're sleeping here. You can have the bed. There's some spare blankets and pillows."

Lorne shook his head. "I couldn't possibly, Alpha."

Jonathan gazed at him in amusement. "Sleep in here or in the bed?"

"Both?" Lorne returned his smile.

Jonathan stood up. "Well, this alpha says you're taking the bed."

"I thought you didn't go in for all that nonsense," Lorne shot back.

Jonathan laughed. "Okay, you got me." He went to the cupboard where he'd seen the blankets and the pillow and pulled them out. Then the bathroom. When he got back, Lorne had made him a bed up on the floor using the comforter as a mattress. A single blanket was on the bed. Jonathan frowned.

"Or I take the floor," Lorne warned.

"That wasn't what I meant," Jonathan said in exasperation. He looked at the bed. Lorne would freeze with just one blanket. There wasn't a spare ounce of fat on him. And there he went again thinking of a naked Lorne, a very stunning naked Lorne. "I have a better idea. We both take the bed." He could behave. Much as he wanted to spend the night getting to see more of a naked Lorne, he would never use the current scenario to his advantage. Above all else, he wanted Lorne to feel safe.

Lorne's eyes widened.

"It's big enough. Look," Jonathan took a breath, "I live and work in this area. I'm not some weirdo that preys on unsuspecting omegas—"

Lorne went crimson, and Jonathan felt like shit. He was going to tell him he was a doctor but whatever. He bent down and rearranged the covers on the bed. Then he got in and rolled away from where he knew Lorne was standing. He counted almost another five seconds before he felt Lorne get in bed.

"How do you know I'm not some weird omega that preys on unsuspecting alphas?"

Jonathan grinned. He'd take his chances.

TWO

LORNE WAS HAVING the most amazing dream. He was toasty warm. The mattress seemed to have magically changed into the softest one ever, and the slight rise and fall was soothing. He—

Lorne froze. *Slight rise and fall?* Everything came back to him in a rush. The alpha. The kind, generous stranger who had shared his bed; Lorne was actually using him *as* a bed. The alpha he was currently sprawled all over. The one he shared a good meal with, and an even better beer, which meant Lorne was out like a light as soon as he'd lain down. Lorne burned with embarrassment and tried to work out how to move without waking Jonathan up because it was obvious the alpha was still asleep. He shifted cautiously, but Jonathan muttered something unintelligible and tightened his arms around him.

Crap.

Now what did he do?

Lie here and dream it would be his new life? Lorne nearly snorted. He didn't need another alpha. Yesterday he would never have even conceived of being happy somewhere else, of another life, but sometime during the seemingly endless cab ride, he'd grown a spine. And he wouldn't let someone treat him like that ever again. People weren't disposable, whether they were omegas or not.

But he would miss his babies. And they were his, no matter what anyone else said. He hoped Sophie managed to get her school project done without his chiding. She was the forgetful one, scatty, but wicked intelligent. Suzanna was the gentlest child he had ever met. She hated that he never ate with the family. A good two thirds of the drawings on his wall were from her. Sophie didn't give him as many, but only because she was as much a perfectionist with her art as she was with everything else.

Nicholas had given him cards every birthday and Christmas for years. It had been Nicholas who had wheedled out of him when his birthday was, and only because Lorne had admitted his seventeenth had been the day he was mated to his father. It had also been Nicholas who, despite his father's disapproval, had continued to buy the cards even when university had meant Lorne didn't often see him.

Although, that was more likely due to Nicholas's barely concealed dislike for his step-mother, and he doubted very much Nicholas would be coming back to live at home permanently. Or remodeling the top floor for an office.

Lorne breathed out. He knew he needed to move, but just for a second, he enjoyed the closeness of another person. Suzanna always gave him lots of hugs when neither her mom nor dad were watching, and he'd never especially felt deprived. He concentrated on working out the best way to move then became aware of another problem.

He was hard. He was hard, and his very obvious erection was currently poking into Jonathan's side.

Oh God. He whimpered in the back of his throat. He had to move. He had to— He realized the gentle rise and fall of Jonathan's chest had stopped. He tried to move away and heard a noisy exhale as Jonathan opened his arms.

"Sorry," Jonathan muttered. "I'm afraid my control isn't as good when I'm asleep."

And Lorne slid back, putting a little distance between them. Then he processed what Jonathan had said. *Control.* Control was the same as discipline. Did that mean he had to stop himself from touching Lorne? A completely giddy thought entered his head. This was the start of his new life. His body finally belonged to him. He was past the age where he had to worry about getting pregnant—the reason for the omega suppressants—and he was damn horny. He was lying in bed with a gorgeous alpha he had been too tired to appreciate last night, but this was morning. And his body was definitely appreciating all that alpha yumminess this morning.

Did he dare? "Control isn't always a good thing," he whispered and screwed his eyes shut tight while he died a little inside. He felt Jonathan still then roll onto his side to face him. He didn't dare breathe. A thumb ghosted his cheek then a finger settled under his chin to draw his head up a little.

"Look at me." The command was quiet but definitive.

Lorne opened his eyes while wishing a lightning bolt would smite him or something, but somehow, looking into his gray eyes wasn't as scary as he imagined. Although the lightning bolt was still a possibility.

"I told you last night you were safe."

"Maybe I don't want to be," Lorne rushed out, completely stunned at his daring.

"I would never, ever want you to think anything I promise comes with conditions, and I'm not looking to mate an omega," Jonathan said. To his credit, he winced a little as he said it.

"Good, because I'm not looking for another alpha," Lorne said with a little more courage.

Jonathan's eyes widened, but a smile hovered on his lips. "And you don't have one now?"

Lorne shook his head, and Jonathan's smile deepened. Without another word, he bent down and settled his lips on Lorne's.

And they were perfect. Softness and strength wrapped up in one delicious package. A little like the arms that pressed against his back, and a lot like the body he was drawn up against. He moaned as Jonathan's tongue licked the ridge of his lips, coaxing them open, then he gently bit down on his lower one, sending a frisson of pleasure straight to his groin.

Jonathan rolled onto his back, taking Lorne with him. His fingers threaded themselves through Lorne's hair as the kiss deepened. Lorne instinctively pressed into him, the delicious ache in his groin almost painful, but so damn good.

"What do you like?" Jonathan murmured as he trailed small nips down his throat with his teeth then soothed them with his tongue.

"Everything you're doing," Lorne replied, wondering why he was being asked.

Jonathan hummed in approval. "So, bottom, top?"

"Bottom," Lorne replied instantly. The thought of being pinned down by this alpha made his cock harden even more.

"I can do either if it's been a while," Jonathan murmured which made Lorne pause.

"I thought Alphas always topped?" The question was out before he even thought about it.

Jonathan smiled. "Nope. I just thought if it had been a while for you, it might hurt."

"A while?" Then Lorne reddened, suddenly understanding what Jonathan was saying. In his defense, the kisses were making his head spin, but there was no way he was telling Jonathan he was a virgin. That the omega suppressants he'd taken for years had been pointless because even if he'd had the inclination, he would never have had the time. "Yes, you might need to take it slow. It's been a while," and he lifted his head in invitation. Jonathan's gray eyes darkened, and he took his lips in a blistering kiss. He broke off.

"Well, the beauty of being snowed in is that we can take our time." Then he paused. "I have to ask how old you are? I don't have any condoms."

"Thirty-three," Lorne replied promptly. He knew Jonathan was asking if he was still fertile. Sexually transmitted diseases had been eradicated a few hundred years ago, but omegas could still get pregnant.

But not him, *never him*. Not any longer.

Jonathan obviously relaxed, and again, Lorne pushed away the slight disappointment. He wasn't thinking about that now. Nothing would spoil what was finally going to happen.

"Turn over," Jonathan instructed and pulled a couple of pillows down for Lorne to lie against. Lorne moved eagerly. He was so hard. The other advantage of finishing his omega suppressants.

Jonathan peppered kisses on his back, his shoulders, and trailed his lips down Lorne's spine. Little shivers ran all over his skin, making him feel alive, almost wanted, if only for a few minutes.

"You are so gorgeous," Jonathan murmured in between kisses, and really, if Jonathan needed a seduction scene, he was saying all the right things. Not that Lorne was going anywhere.

Jonathan shuffled lower, his lips now reaching Lorne's lower back, his hands moving to cradle Lorne's hips. "Lift up a little onto your knees."

Lorne paused for a second. He knew, of course he knew, but it made him feel so exposed, so vulnerable. Jonathan obviously sensed his hesitation. "We don't have to. We—"

And because Jonathan had told him he didn't have to, Lorne immediately moved. Jonathan chuckled and knelt up behind him. "Just because I wanted to do this," he murmured and dipped his head. Lorne's cock registered the exquisite pleasure faster than he did, and it swelled and pulsed.

Lorne whimpered. "Stop."

Jonathan immediately stilled and raised his head. "Of course. Are you okay?"

Lorne fumbled for his cock and squeezed the end as hard as he could bear. "I—I'm sorry."

Jonathan smoothed one hand from the base of his neck to his ass. Lorne shuddered. "What's wrong? Do you want me to stop?"

"I-I'm so close, and there's the pillows, and you aren't, and..."

Lorne trailed off and buried his head. His ass was in the air, and he just wanted to curl up and die somewhere else. Somewhere he couldn't be seen. What had he been thinking?

Jonathan got off the bed and went to the bathroom. Lorne immediately moved and curled up in a ball. He could sleep on the floor. He wouldn't even be cold now that his face was on fire.

"Ah, sweetheart," Jonathan murmured, and Lorne opened his eyes. Jonathan was standing holding the towels they had used earlier. He bent and brushed a kiss on Lorne's parted lips. "You had a good thought. I got so carried away by how gorgeous you are I never completely thought it through."

"You—" *Gorgeous? He thinks I'm gorgeous?* Lorne was so stunned he didn't register Jonathan getting back in to bed until he was gathered up in his arms and kissed senseless. And then he forgot his embarrassment, forgot everything, as Jonathan gently coaxed him until he was hard again. Kissed him fiercely, breathlessly, but so tenderly Lorne could have cried. They laughed when Lorne hissed at the cold lube, but he forgot completely once the smooth fingers followed. It hurt—of course it did—but he'd barely felt it before Jonathan's soft murmurs and sweet touches chased it away to be replaced by an ache that grew so big it surrounded him. Then Jonathan was inside. Filling him. Overpowering him as a wave of lust and ecstasy crashed through him, leaving nothing behind except the whispers of utter and real contentment. He barely felt Jonathan gather him close, and the last tender kiss that lulled him to sleep.

Lorne woke to the noise of the bath filling and an empty bed, but before he'd had the chance to even think of anything being awkward, Jonathan—a very naked Jonathan—walked out of the bathroom. Lorne tried to swallow down a very dry throat, and his body, which had been toasty warm, became engulfed in heat, even the parts that were a little sore this morning.

"Good morning." Jonathan smiled and walked over. "I ran a bath."

Does he know? Did he know it had been Lorne's first time? It wasn't like he had a big V stamped on his forehead. Jonathan held his hand out wordlessly, and Lorne was helpless to do anything other than take it. The room was warm, but he was pleased to see the large steaming bath. Then he had another shock as Jonathan stepped in and sat down. "There's room for both of us."

Lorne felt the smile on his face grow wider, and in a few seconds, he was sitting in between Jonathan's legs and leaning back against his chest.

"Mmm. I was supposed to be on a beach right about now. My first vacation in nearly three years, but I've never been so glad to be snowed in in my life."

Lorne didn't tell him he'd never had a vacation. He'd traveled with the family, but with no housekeeper or cleaning service, he'd worked harder than he had at home. He'd had one day on the beach when the alpha and his wife had gone to meet friends, and he'd stayed with Nicholas and the girls. It had been one of the best days of his life, and Nicholas had even taught him how to catch the fish they had grilled for supper.

Jonathan squeezed some soap onto a sponge and proceeded to gently wash him all over. He shivered when Jonathan brushed his nipples, and Jonathan chuckled. "Mmm, that's something we can explore later." He didn't try and touch his hole, which Lorne was secretly glad of because he was a little sore, but he very thoroughly washed his cock and balls until his cock was jutting up to attention out of the water. Of course, that seemed to amuse Jonathan, and he lavished more attention on it until Lorne was trying not to squirm.

"Relax," Jonathan murmured. "Don't try and hold back. I want you to enjoy it."

"You're spoiling me," Lorne gasped, only to have Jonathan angle his head so he could kiss Lorne as he came.

"Something tells me you deserve it," Jonathan said quietly as he rinsed him carefully afterwards. Jonathan steadied Lorne because his knees were like jelly then wrapped him in big fluffy towels to dry, and Lorne had to bite his lip to stop blurting out his thanks. He'd expected—at least—to be treated with consideration last night. It never occurred to him once that Jonathan had any other motives for inviting him upstairs other than compassion. Jonathan was a good-looking alpha and certainly would be able to take his pick of lovers. But this morning had shocked him. To be cared for so lovingly—

Lovingly. What was he thinking? Jonathan was simply a nice guy. Just because his own alpha had been an ass didn't mean he should assign courtesy and consideration any deeper meaning, and he certainly needed to stop himself from getting carried away.

"I'm going to go down and find us some breakfast." Jonathan pulled his pants on. "Then we can eat in bed." He waggled his eyebrows, and Lorne couldn't help laughing. He opened the door and bent down, picking up a pile of laundry. "Your pants," he smiled and passed them over. Then he leaned down and took a hot hurried kiss that made Lorne's toes curl and walked out, closing the door behind him.

Lorne reached over and picked up the sweater Jonathan had tossed on the bed along with Lorne's pants. It was a dark blue, and Lorne pressed it to his face. It didn't smell of Jonathan now it had been laundered, but it reminded him of him. He lowered the sweater to his lap, licked his lips, and ignored the tightness in his belly that usually accompanied the thought he might have forgotten something or said the wrong thing because he hadn't. And even if he had, Jonathan would have forgiven him. He knew that. The alpha had been nothing but kind, gentle, and considerate.

And Lorne was falling for him. *Hard.*

And that was so dangerous. No alpha would want a retired omega. One whose body couldn't have the babies every alpha wanted, and even if Jonathan wanted what...an affair? Jonathan had made it clear he wasn't looking for an omega. Maybe he was one of the new types that just wanted a wife or a husband. He'd heard it happened now in some of the big cities. In one of his alpha's newspapers, he'd seen some scientists were even predicting fertile male omegas wouldn't be born anymore in a few hundred years. That natural evolution would progress. After all, their original purpose was to increase a threatened population after the great wars, not to become an unpaid servant for whoever could afford one.

But he guessed that had become lost in the last few centuries.

And whatever Jonathan intended, he knew it absolutely wouldn't include him. Lorne nearly leaped out of bed and rushed to get dressed. He had to go. He'd survived being rejected by the family he thought was his, but he knew he absolutely wouldn't survive it a second time.

He knew his rented room was around a mile away, and he'd managed to walk seven in a blizzard yesterday. He could manage another one now.

THREE

SIX MONTHS LATER

JONATHAN LOOKED AWAY from where he was studying the x-rays of what was clearly a broken wrist as the curtain opened and Roger walked into the empty bay. The registrar glanced at the screen and frowned. "What are you thinking?"

Jonathan shook his head. "You mean apart from me wanting to take a baseball bat to the alpha who did this?"

Roger sighed. "He's not saying anything, but he's clearly nervous of the alpha who brought him in."

"How old is the omega?"

The registrar opened the folder he was carrying. "Shay Nicholls, nineteen and approximately three months pregnant. Mated to Devin Jones. He has no other breaks, but he's underweight and has a few bruises on his upper arms. He became a little distressed when I insisted on an internal exam. I couldn't help noticing what looked like blood and confirmed he has some anal tearing."

Jonathan cursed.

"I insisted on admitting him tonight, but I have no authority to keep him any longer."

Jonathan clicked off the viewer. "Make sure Trixie or Jill is assigned to him. And ensure he has time to talk to them alone."

Roger's eyebrows rose, but he didn't comment. The law wasn't very strict on the treatment of omegas, and unless an omega could prove he was being physically abused, there was nothing the authorities could or would do. Even then, it wasn't easy. There had been some talk of an organization to help them, and Jonathan was sure at least two of the nurses were involved, but so far, none of them trusted him enough to tell him anything.

Not that he blamed them. He was newer here and an alpha after all. Trust took time.

"I actually wanted you to see a new patient," Roger said. "I certainly have no experience with this. I didn't even know it was possible—"

"What?" Jonathan interrupted intrigued.

"Elderly prima gravida. Male omega."

Jonathan winced. He hoped Roger didn't use that term around the patient. Prima gravida meant first pregnancy, and in females, technically elderly could refer to anyone over the age of thirty-five. Of course that was impossible in an omega.

"How old?"

"Thirty-three."

Jonathan's eyebrows lifted. "Are you sure?" Male omegas weren't fertile after the age of thirty, and even then, in the last few years before they reached thirty, pregnancy was rare and keeping a child to term was even rarer. The pouch designed to replicate a female uterus would degenerate over the course of the years, and only remained viable for around twenty-five, thirty at the absolute maximum.

"To be honest, I think he's got the dates wrong, but he's insisting he's twenty-five weeks, and he's been forced to check in with us because he says he can't eat."

"You think he's further on?" Jonathan followed Roger out to the waiting area.

"Yes, by quite a lot. If you saw him, you would think he was due.

Anyway, he's here because he knows he needs the nutrition supplements, so I've just sent him for a scan. He says he's just moved to the area, and his alpha hasn't had him see anyone about his pregnancy so far."

Jonathan frowned. That wasn't uncommon either. Omegas often presented only when they were forced to come for the nutritional supplements for their last month. The small passage that only opened during birth was so close to the rectum it was normally completely sealed. Male omegas were given pills to stop them producing normal waste from thirty weeks on when their rectum closed to make space, and they obviously couldn't eat real food. If there was any question over dates, the patient would always be sent for a scan. "What's his alpha saying?"

Roger glanced at him uncomfortably. "He hasn't got anyone with him. Says his alpha is too busy. The nurse didn't push because she was frightened he would just leave."

Which was true. If there was a chance this omega was unmated, the authorities would simply remove the child. They both walked past reception and into the imaging bay. Jonathan and Roger let themselves in to the viewing area so as not to interrupt the technician or distress the patient by having an audience.

Roger turned on the screen so they could see what the technician was seeing. The screen flickered then focused.

Jonathan's lips parted in surprise, and Roger gaped in shock. "That's impossible."

It would also explain why Roger thought the omega was further along than he insisted. Jonathan nodded, pressed the intercom, and quietly asked to see the technician when she was done. He knew the technician wouldn't tell the patient the news because she would know how serious it was. That would be left to Roger—or Jonathan now because he was definitely taking this case. He watched the technician take measurements of the fetuses. *All of them.* Because Jonathan could clearly see three little bodies and count three heart beats. This omega, already at risk because he was pregnant in the first place, was having triplets.

And there was a very high chance he could lose all of them before they were even born.

Lorne closed his eyes as the technician moved the wand gently over his belly and concentrated on not letting a tear escape from beneath his eyelids. He knew there was something really wrong. He was way too big for how many weeks he was. He'd spent weeks doing nothing more than reading up on omega pregnancies and looking at pictures. It wasn't uncommon to hardly be able to tell male omegas were pregnant until the last few weeks. Male omegas usually delivered around thirty-six weeks, sometimes earlier, and the whole process was so much more risky than for females. But in the years following the great wars, they needed all alpha females to work to get the world functioning again instead of having babies, and in their male dominated society, there simply weren't enough beta or omega females left to go around. He supposed it had seemed a good idea at the time.

And he had been so ecstatic when he had found out. So completely stunned when everything else he'd tried to stop feeling nauseous hadn't worked and he'd finally succumbed and bought a pregnancy test at the local store. There had even been a sweet lady called Annabel who had helped him pick one out. She'd been so discreet, and he'd really wanted to become friends with her, especially after she had told him proudly her son Matthew was an omega.

But he simply hadn't dared. Because it was obvious he was living on his own. And as the only males who could get pregnant were omegas, he might get reported. And there was nothing he wouldn't do to protect this baby. He knew he would have to move after he or she was born and invent a cover story, but by then, no one would know he had actually given birth. It was only the sight of him being pregnant that would raise questions now. He'd decide how to invent a fictitious alpha later.

And Annabel's father-in-law had even delivered groceries for him on the small electric cart his family had given him to drive because his eyesight wasn't good enough for anything that could go faster than fifteen miles an hour. He didn't think George would have even noticed he was pregnant.

The technician clicked the monitor off, and Lorne felt more tears well. She hadn't said anything. She hadn't invited him to look at the screen, and she hadn't asked him if he wanted to know if he was having a girl or boy. His heart, which had seemed to sink to his toes, now resurfaced and was pounding so hard it could easily break his ribs. He felt a tissue pressed into his palm. "I'll let you get dressed, Mr. Austin. Please take your time, and the doctor will see you in the office over there when you are done." She squeezed his hand, and Lorne felt a tear escape.

Lorne waited until he heard the door close before he opened his eyes. He had to roll slightly to sit up, but he had to get up and go to the bathroom because the water they had made him drink was playing havoc with his already squashed bladder. He wanted to ask so many questions, but he didn't know where to start. His baby was alive—and kicking—he knew that, but there had to be something really wrong.

He gingerly bent, got dressed, and made it with relief to the bathroom then came back to the room where he had been scanned. There was a small office next to it, and he assumed that was where he was seeing the doctor. He felt a little shaky—a lot shaky—as he worked his way there. One of the reasons he had been forced to come was he simply couldn't eat and not fueling his body was putting them both at risk. He didn't think he'd managed more than a bite for the last week, and even then, he'd thrown it up. He was desperate.

He knocked at the office door and heard a deep voice bid him to come in. He opened the door and looked over just as the doctor in the white coat raised his head with a smile.

And what seemed like every bit of blood in his body rushed to his boots. He heard the exclamation from what seemed like a million miles away before he fell headlong into a dark tunnel that swallowed him up.

LORNE OPENED HIS EYES, feeling distinctly nauseous, and for a few seconds, he didn't know where he was or why someone seemed to be holding his hand. No *wrist*, and with a sinking heart, he closed them again to avoid seeing the one man he had never thought to meet again.

Still too damn good looking. And what were the chances? What had he possibly done in a former life that would rain down such bad luck on him? He felt a familiar thumb brush the side of his cheek.

"Lorne?"

He opened his eyes and swallowed uncomfortably, taking in the hospital bed he was lying in and the IV line running into his arm. Jonathan sat down next to him and covered one of his hands. "Why did you disappear?"

Lorne started in surprise. It hadn't been the question he was expecting. He tried to swallow again, but Jonathan passed him the glass of water and angled the straw. He didn't let go, simply holding it patiently while Lorne eased his throat.

Lorne let go of the straw, and Jonathan put it back on the side table. He sat back down and covered Lorne's hand again with one of his own. Lorne knew he should move his own hand, but he couldn't dredge up the strength.

"Tell me what's wrong," Lorne begged, completely ignoring Jonathan's question.

And Jonathan nodded. "Okay. Firstly congratulations. As I'm sure you know, you are pretty much six months pregnant. The scan would confirm the dates you have given of twenty-five weeks. I'm sure you also know that this is one for the history books."

Lorne raised alarmed eyes, and Jonathan's swept over him. "I know you're worried and realize the consequences, and I will explain everything, but obviously, I have a question first."

"Yes," Lorne said. There was no point denying the baby was Jonathan's. A simple DNA test would confirm it, even if they hadn't already done that.

"And why didn't you tell me? You could have gotten my address from Harry or Molly."

Lorne gazed at him. He didn't seem angry. But then he didn't need to be. He could take the baby or give it up to the authorities for adoption. Either way he would lose it. "Because you said you didn't want an omega."

Jonathan smiled. "*Ah*. Well, yes, I suppose that would explain it."

"How is it possible I'm even pregnant?" He'd been stunned to find out.

"We've done some early bloodwork." He paused. "Were you ever given omega suppressants?"

Lorne nodded. "The alpha never wanted me to get pregnant. His wife had the children, but they were my responsibility straight after." He said that with a touch of defiance.

"So they were used as a contraceptive?" Jonathan said flatly.

Lorne frowned. "No. He never—" Then he blushed realizing what he was admitting to.

"Are you telling me you never had sex with your alpha?" Lorne nodded but didn't look at Jonathan. Another few seconds passed. "When did you stop taking them?"

Then he did look up. "About five weeks before we met. I didn't bother ordering any more because it was pointless when I knew my mating contract would be finishing soon. I'd been instructed to just continue them after I arrived at the omega offices—"

"Continue?"

Jonathan nodded. "My mom and dad gave me them to me from about fourteen." He shrugged. "Alpha Carmichael said I had to continue for the full term of the contract, so I just included them in the grocery shopping every week."

Jonathan shook his head. "I don't understand why you would be made to take them if he didn't intend them for contraception."

But Lorne did. There had been a scandal with one of their friends. A female omega had gotten pregnant with a boy she had met at the local store even before she had been mated. They had been secretly meeting for months, and it was only when she couldn't hide the pregnancy she had confessed. The alpha was backed into a corner. They were mated, so he had to raise the child. He knew the mistress had no intention of having it happen to them. Lorne nearly huffed. As if he would ever have had the chance.

"But we think, after taking them for so long, suddenly stopping caused a spike in your hormones, resulting in an immediate pregnancy...and something else."

Lorne stopped breathing. He didn't dare ask.

"An older mom having a multiple pregnancy is more common that you think."

Lorne frowned. "What has that to do with me?"

"We think the same principle applies. Technically, you are classed as an older mom, *dad*," he smiled. "And along with the hormone spike we think that caused it."

Wait. *Multiple.* Multiple birth. "I'm having twins?" Lorne whispered in complete awe.

"I wish it was that simple," Jonathan said gravely. "You're having triplets. Two boys and one girl."

It was a good thing Lorne was lying down, or he would have probably passed out a second time. "Triplets?" Lorne squeaked out.

Jonathan nodded. Jonathan's eyes shone in excitement for a second then they dimmed, and Lorne understood. It didn't matter how many babies he was having. He still wouldn't be keeping any of them, and he slid his hand out from under Jonathan's.

"So we have some decisions to make," Jonathan said gently. Lorne closed his eyes not wanting to hear.

"I know I have to give them up. Unmated omegas—"

"Stop," Jonathan took hold of his hand. "I have an attorney drawing up a mating contract as we speak." He smiled. "The sister of a very good friend of mine actually."

"A mating contract?" Lorne must be hearing things.

Jonathan paused. "I figured after fighting so hard to keep them you wouldn't want to give them up?"

Lorne shook his head in a complete daze. "But—"

"I don't want an omega?" Jonathan finished the sentence.

"Yes."

"I did say that, and it's true I don't want an unpaid servant, but taking responsibility for a family I helped to create is a whole other thing."

Lorne watched as wonder curved Jonathan's lips, hardly believing what he was hearing. Jonathan was offering him everything he had ever wanted. He was including him very generously in the package deal. He could just take the babies. Have his wife... "Are you married?"

Jonathan shook his head. "No, absolutely not."

"You said a couple of things." Would they live together?

Jonathan grew serious and very deliberately retook Lorne's hand. Lorne's heart started beating faster. "I've asked for a specialist to look at you. You realize this pregnancy is incredibly risky and you may need specialist care? I trained years ago with a professor of obstetrics, and we became friends. He's flying up and will look at you tomorrow."

Lorne sat up. He would need to get dressed, go home, and gather some clothes. "Whoa," Jonathan said, putting a hand on Lorne's shoulder. "What are you doing?"

"I—"

"Okay, that *wasn't* a question. What I meant to say was you are staying right here. At least until Professor Denholm has seen you tomorrow. You are allowed out of bed, accompanied, to go to the bathroom and that is it. You feel one twinge, see a speck of blood, you even *stub your toe,* and I want to know about it imme-diately."

Lorne's lips parted, ready to speak, but as he'd no idea what to say, he closed them again.

"Good decision," Jonathan said in amusement. "I'm sending in a nurse called Trixie who's going to make you a lot more comfortable while I do my rounds, and we're moving you to a private room."

"Why?" was all Lorne could think to say, and Jonathan smiled.

"Because you're mine, and from this second on, you're going to be spoiled." Lorne inhaled sharply to stop the threat of tears. His hormones had been ridiculous. He'd cry at the drop of a hat.

"But you don't know me," he said in complete bewilderment.

"You came because you would rather risk having to say goodbye to your babies than cause them harm. I don't need to know anything else right at this minute." Very gently, Jonathan wiped the moisture out from under his eyelids and bent and brushed a soft kiss on his lips.

FOUR

JONATHAN'S own knees were very wobbly as he left Lorne's room. He'd been stunned to see Lorne, but thankfully, he'd noticed the color leach from his face and made it around the desk to catch him before he hit the floor.

A family. Jonathan took a steadying breath. *If they lived.* He knew realistically the chances were little above zero, and he had no idea what to say to Lorne. Although Lorne didn't seem unintelligent. He would have to be smart to last this long on his own without getting reported.

Nana would be thrilled. He knew she despaired of him ever settling down as she put it, but he disagreed on principle with alphas "owning" omegas like possessions, and he'd only ever been close to getting married once.

He shook off all thoughts of that and went to find the head nurse to start his rounds. He also wanted to visit the omega Roger was treating and see if he could help. He was on his third patient of the day when Roger caught up to him. "Sorry. I was trying to persuade Shay Nicholls to stay."

"Stay?" Jonathan stepped away from Mrs. Jennings who was fussing over Dana, her omega. "What do you mean *stay?*"

"His alpha turned up thirty minutes ago and told him he would 'probably' be more comfortable at home," Roger said sardonically. "Shay took the hint and immediately said he was leaving. We have no authority to detain him, so I just said he was due in the clinic on Monday."

Jonathan closed his eyes briefly. He hated having his hands tied, but he had to be careful. If Shay's alpha got one hint they were critical of him, it would be the last they saw of Shay. There were other omega clinics and other doctors who wouldn't care as much. "Let me know the second he appears on Monday or if he doesn't." He would do a damn home visit if he had to.

An hour later, he was in his office and debating whether to get some lunch or go see Lorne. He'd just spoken to Trixie who reported Lorne was asleep, so he didn't want to rush in and wake him.

His cell phone rang, and Jonathan answered it.

"Jonathan, my boy!"

Jonathan grinned but held the phone a little farther away from his ear drums. "Professor Denholm. Thank you for returning my call so quickly."

He heard the chuckle down the phone. "And I told you to call me Gregory," he scolded.

Jonathan smiled. "I have a patient I would really appreciate an urgent consult on."

"Yes?" Gregory was suddenly all business, and Jonathan told him Lorne's brief details. He heard Gregory sigh.

"I might be experienced, Jonathan, but not even I can perform miracles."

Jonathan sighed. He knew, but hearing it from someone else made it ten times worse. "The omega is in good health normally," he added.

"Hmm." Gregory pondered. "There may be something I can

suggest, but I would need to see the young man in question first. How supportive is his alpha?"

There was a silence. Jonathan cleared his throat. "I'll do whatever is best for Lorne."

Gregory started chuckling. "Well, well. What happened to the revolutionary intern I had who insisted omegas weren't mere chattel?"

"It's complicated," Jonathan sighed. "But yeah, I'll do anything to keep him, *them*, safe."

"Very good," Gregory said. "I can be there in under two hours."

"Really? I thought you were in Capital City?" Which was either an overnight drive or a good plane ride away.

"No, we're visiting my daughter Marianna who just got a teaching position up here. Met a beta the same day, and they're getting married in the spring. Nice girl called Rachel. An artist. Has a shop. Obviously, the wife is making immediate noises about us living too far away if we get grandbabies. I just reminded her about this sector's wicked snowstorms, but I think, between the wife and Marianna, I'm going to be doing what I'm told."

Jonathan smiled, despite having his fears confirmed. "It would be good to see you more often."

Gregory huffed. "You just want the wife's cherry cobbler."

"It would be good to see you more often, sir," Jonathan amended, "but it would be even better if that included a dinner invitation."

"And I forgot to ask. How's that grandmother of yours?"

It was Jonathan's turn to sigh. "Stubborn. Won't consider anything other than living in that old house. I'm terrified every day I'm going to get a call saying she fell down the stairs."

"Well you tried, Jonathan. I'll get the wife to give her a call. See if we can knock some sense into her together."

They chatted for another couple of minutes then Gregory said Michael had brought the car back, so they would see him soon and hung up.

Jonathan scrubbed his face. He knew what Gregory was going to say to Lorne, and he knew it would kill him. He also knew if Lorne had any chance of keeping even one baby, it may be all they could hope for. He was also a coward and extremely relieved it would be Gregory giving Lorne the bad news and not him.

LORNE WAS AWAKE. He'd heard the door open and the quiet words from Trixie telling Jonathan all his vitals were good and he'd stayed in bed. He opened his eyes to Jonathan's amused gray ones as he felt the bed dip. "I knew you weren't asleep."

Lorne couldn't even dredge up a smile. He was scared—*terrified.* And just because Jonathan had offered to mate him for the sake of the babies didn't necessarily mean he was doing the right thing. He felt like he was being backed into a corner, but worse still, that Jonathan was. And that it would only lead to resentment and unhappiness. Jonathan would resent being tied to a pathetic—

"Hey." Lorne focused on the large hand covering his own. "I know you're scared, but I will do my very best to look after all of you."

He looked up, tears clogging his throat. He was such a wuss. "I-I never intended to force you into anything."

"Oh, I know." Jonathan shook his head in what seemed mild exasperation. "I tried to find you a few times. I came back to the pub regularly, but Harry never saw you again, and no one had your address."

"Why?" Lorne blurted out. "You knew I was an omega and—"

"Never have my words come back to bite me on the butt so thoroughly." Jonathan interrupted. "But none of that matters, because you're here now."

He was. But they were still together because the law was forcing them to be.

"So, tell me a little about you. You said you were moving into the area but not why."

So Lorne did. He told Jonathan everything.

"You're gonna miss them." He meant his babies. His *other* babies.

"I thought about writing, but I'm kind of worried Nicholas might want to visit and—" He clamped his lips closed, but it was too late.

"Why would Nicholas visiting upset you? I would have thought you would love to see them."

Lorne nodded. What did he say?

Jonathan's eyes narrowed. He was far too astute. "I wondered if you trusted me enough to give me your house keys?"

Yep, way too astute.

"Why?" Lorne asked.

"You mean apart from the fact you are now living with me and we need to get your things?" Jonathan smiled. Lorne loved his smile. The way his eyes crinkled at the corners and the dimple at the side of his lips. His very kissable lips.

"I'm living with you?"

Jonathan tilted his head as if he was puzzled. "Of course."

Of course.

"I live in an old house that needs tearing down I'm afraid, but we can get something more child-friendly later."

Lorne shook his head. He was still asleep and dreaming. Jonathan held his hand out, and Lorne nodded to the jacket over his chair. Jonathan stood up and retrieved them from the pocket. He got out his phone. "Tell me your address, and I'll take care of it."

So Lorne did then, feeling brave, dared a question. "Do you have any family?"

Jonathan nodded. "I have a stubborn seventy-five-year-old grand-mother who lives with me. The house is completely unsuitable, and I hate living there. I've offered to get her a house of her own or a new one with me, and she flatly refuses, so I can't move either."

Lorne's eyebrows rose enquiringly, and Jonathan sighed. "She's too old to be living alone in that mausoleum. I've suggested one of those new apartments down by the river, but she says they're for old people." He grinned. "We're at an impasse."

Trixie came back in to change his IV bag.

"You won't need an IV by tomorrow," Jonathan explained. "You can move to the oral supplements, but your levels were all too low, so we're giving you a boost." He stood up. "How long has it been since you managed to eat anything?"

Lorne watched as Jonathan transitioned into doctor mode, including asking some embarrassing questions. Trixie left the room.

"Now," Jonathan asked. "Do you want to go to the bathroom before she gets back and insists on taking you?'

Lorne nodded, not surprised in the least Jonathan had guessed how he felt.

"Then I'll make you a deal. I'll take you if you'll lie down and try and get some more rest after you're done. The doctor I told you about is much nearer than I thought, so he'll be in to see you in about an hour." He brushed a finger along the length of Lorne's cheek. "I know it's hard, but please try not to worry. That's not going to help any of you."

Lorne nodded, and slowly, with Jonathan's help, he got out of bed. Then he stilled as someone made their presence felt.

"What is it?" Jonathan said in alarm.

Lorne smiled. "Someone's kicking."

Jonathan's lips parted. "Can I feel?"

"Of course." Lorne took Jonathan's hand and placed it over where someone seemed to be trying to do a somersault. Lorne watched as Jonathan's expression changed from serious to wonder-ous. Awe shining from his eyes.

"That's incredible."

"But you must have felt it a million times," Lorne protested.

"But not mine," Jonathan said quietly and met Lorne's gaze. And Lorne was glad Jonathan still had one hand under his arm because he could have melted on the spot. "It's also incredible because they don't have as much room to move."

"Maybe he's elbowing his brother and sister out of the way."

Jonathan huffed. "Oh no, I'd bet money that's the girl bossing her brothers around." Lorne gazed at Jonathan, watching the smile play on his lips. Then the smile fell, and Lorne knew he was thinking the same as he was.

"What if I lose them?" He choked out. Life was so cruel. He'd been happy with his life, only to lose everything in the space of an afternoon. And he'd thought, when he found out he was pregnant by some miracle, he was getting a second chance.

Jonathan eased Lorne forward into his arms which wasn't that easy. "Let's not think that way. Let's wait and see what our options are. Professor Denholm will be here soon."

Jonathan helped Lorne to the bathroom and even gave him a few minutes privacy, despite—Lorne was sure—Jonathan not wanting to let him out of his sight. Jonathan got called away to see another patient shortly after, and Trixie came back in to check he was okay. He liked the bubbly, blond-haired nurse.

"You do know you're single-handedly responsible for breaking every nurse's heart here, don't you?" she confided after refreshing his water and shutting the blinds, urging him to take a nap.

Lorne waited for the explanation.

"Everyone adores Dr. Owens. All the moms or the omegas want him to deliver their baby, and you're having *his* babies." She put a hand to her heart and sighed dramatically. "He only started working here last fall, and he's already got all the nurses fighting over him."

She bustled about some more, not noticing Lorne hadn't replied, before she urged him again to get some rest and promised to wake him before the professor arrived.

Everyone adores Dr. Owens? What was it about him that made Jonathan immediately offer to mate him? He didn't understand why he would be interested in Lorne after the babies were born, but a mating contract guaranteed him at least fifteen years with them.

But then what?

Lorne shook his head. There was no point worrying about something fifteen years in the future when it wasn't even certain— Lorne closed his eyes. He had to stop thinking like that. Worry wasn't good for the babies.

"Mr. Austin?"

Lorne opened his eyes. He must have slept again which surprised him. He smiled at Trixie.

"Professor Denholm is here talking to Dr. Owens. I thought you'd appreciate five minutes before they come in."

Lorne smiled and sat up, immediately noticing the half-drunk cup of what looked like coffee on his bedside table. Trixie followed his gaze and rolled her eyes. "I don't think he's gotten a minute to actually finish a cup all day, and I'm certain he's not had any lunch."

"Who?" Lorne was confused.

"Dr. Owens. He was in here before Professor Denholm arrived."

Lorne paused. He'd been back? And Lorne had been asleep. "Is there any chance I can go to the bathroom?" He needed to pee like usual, and he wanted to brush his teeth.

"Absolutely." Trixie helped him. When he was done, he opened the bathroom door to see his room a little fuller than it had been before. Jonathan smiled and crossed over to him taking his arm.

"Let's get you back in bed then I'll introduce you."

Lorne got in and turned his attention to the older, gray-haired man who was reading his chart but put it down as soon as Lorne was settled and held out his hand. "Mr. Austin, I'm Professor Denholm. Very pleased to meet you."

Lorne shook his hand in a little bit of a daze. He smiled at the other doctor he had met when he arrived and Trixie who hovered in the background.

"Do you mind if I examine you?"

Lorne shook his head, and in a minute, he was lying on his back with his baby bump exposed. The professor smiled and rubbed his hands together to warm them. "No wonder you had everyone questioning your dates, hmm?" And he elbowed Jonathan like he was teasing him.

Jonathan smiled good naturedly, but the look he sent Lorne was filled with heat from their shared memory. Lorne felt his face flushing a little. The professor made some comments to both Jonathan and the other doctor that sounded quite technical but was very gentle when he pressed on with his hands. He got out a stethoscope and listened intently. Lorne waited with bated breath. He desperately wanted to hear his babies himself, but the technician hadn't offered, and it didn't look like the professor was going to either.

Trixie stepped forward to help Lorne sit up afterward, but Jonathan beat her to it and covered him up again. The professor glanced at Trixie and the other doctor. "I think a little privacy if you don't mind." Lorne's pulse picked up as he watched them leave, so much so he barely noticed Jonathan taking his hand.

"Hey," Jonathan chided. "Breathe."

The professor nodded approvingly then surprised Lorne by sitting down on one of the chairs next to the bed. Jonathan perched on the bed next to him. He was pretty sure this wasn't the usual treatment.

"It's bad, isn't it?" he burst out, unable to wait any longer. Jonathan squeezed his hand.

The professor fixed him a steady look. "If Jonathan hadn't given me a brief explanation as to the circumstances, I would be kicking his ass for letting this go so long without raising a number of very large red flags." Lorne flushed, but the professor smiled again. "And I have never found myself in this position, even with the extra twenty or so years of experience in obstetrics, especially omega care, I have on your alpha." He glanced at Jonathan. "I can only offer my opinion as Jonathan has asked me to do. What you chose to do is up to you and Jonathan." Lorne tried to swallow down his dry throat.

"I'm not sure what you have been told or what you are aware of, so I will explain from the beginning. As you know, human males are not built naturally to carry and nurture babies, to say nothing of actually delivering them. But after the wars decimated the population, the human race found itself perilously short of Alpha females, so human male physiology was altered in certain circumstances to enable them to give birth. I believe there was a story associated with a scientist who lost his wife and child, and because of his age, he wasn't allowed to take a second wife when they were in such a short supply, but that may be just one for the romantics among us." The professor's eyes twinkled.

"Certain males were altered, and not just physically, but hormonal supplements in huge quantities were liberally used to shape the development of our omegas. Our society brought in strict laws to manage the Alpha, Beta, omega designations after the great wars to manage the decimated regions with no leadership and little infrastructure. A great deal of advanced technology was destroyed at the same time because the humans who were left blamed a lot of the advances on causing the divisions that existed between the different countries as they were called then." The professor glanced at Jonathan. "As you know, the humans that were left basically rein-vented themselves and the society—the world—we know today is the result."

"The laws were passed at a time when the humans left were panicked," Jonathan added. "And unfortunately, they have never been updated."

The professor nodded. "Which is my usual long-winded way of trying to explain why you are in the position you are in." He glanced at Jonathan again. "And just so you understand, I have not discussed my advice with your alpha. I imagine he may guess at what I'm going to say, but I wanted you both to hear it at the same time, and while I don't want to cause you distress, I have to be honest."

Lorne looked at Jonathan to see his reaction, but his face was expressionless, and he tried to bank down his panic. He knew. He absolutely knew it was going to be bad.

"Your babies—in my opinion—will not survive the pregnancy. I think the stress of three babies on the pouch that is made to nurture only one will result in it tearing from your abdominal wall, and that separation, as you know, would cut off their blood supply which is how they live. The resulting bleed may well threaten your own life.

The pouch was never designed to house a multiple pregnancy, and as far as I am aware, not even twins have been born successfully to male omegas. You are at least three weeks away from them being able to survive on their own judging by their current size, and then it would depend on their condition. I doubt very much if the pouch will be viable for even half that time. Babies have been successfully born a week or two earlier to females, but pregnancies in male omegas are a much higher risk. And there is another complication should you opt to try and wait. The lining is, in my opinion, again judging from the scan, already beginning to separate, meaning the babies are also at risk from being left inside it. Every day increases their risk of not enough oxygenated blood flow to sustain them."

Lorne didn't know he was crying until Jonathan's arm tugged him in close, and he turned his head to press into his shoulder and felt the shirt dampen. Lorne clutched at Jonathan in despair.

"And your advice?" Jonathan asked after a minute.

"Multifetal pregnancy reduction."

Lorne raised his head. "What?"

"And I would suggest you chose the largest to keep. From the scans, the female has the highest chance of survival."

Survival? "I don't understand."

Jonathan turned and pressed his lips to Lorne's head in an apologetic gesture. "It means," he said slowly, "the only way we would have a chance to save one of their lives is to stop the other two developing."

Lorne raised his head in complete horror. He couldn't be serious. "Are you saying," he managed to croak out, "not only are you going to kill two of our babies, but you expect me to choose which one?"

FIVE

LORNE HAD BECOME SO distraught Jonathan had prescribed a mild sedative and stayed with him until he had fallen asleep. He'd been so busy trying to comfort Lorne, Gregory had left with a simple urge to call him when he could.

Not that he was convinced Lorne even knew he was there after a while. He'd turned over on his side, very firmly away from Jonathan, and shut his eyes as guilt lay over Jonathan like a cloud. It was true Gregory hadn't discussed anything with him before he had examined Lorne, but Jonathan wasn't stupid. He was simply a coward and had left it to someone else to deliver the bad news.

And he still didn't know what to say. He knew what he *should* say—of course he did. With his medical hat on, he should already be scheduling the procedure, but instead, he'd waited until he was sure Lorne was asleep, and with a promise from Trixie to call him if Lorne so much as stirred, he had driven to the address Lorne had given him.

It was a store. Jonathan stared in confusion at the small corner shop tucked away at the end of Main street. So small he'd never even noticed it. Not that he spent a lot of time in Granley. He had his groceries delivered, and there was a larger supermarket a mile further on. To be honest, in the seven months since he had been back after he had gotten the panicked call from his gran's neighbor, he done nothing except work. And go to the wedding of course. And then he'd nearly missed it because one of his omegas had gone into premature labor.

Jonathan got out of his car cautiously and walked into the store, not knowing what to say. A middle-aged man looked up as he entered and wished him a good afternoon, enquiring if he could help him find anything.

"Actually, I'm hoping you can tell me how to get to Lorne's room." He brandished a key. The man looked him up and down and gestured behind him.

"Stairs out the back, and you can tell him I want the room back. His alpha stopped sending payments, and he owes me two months. The wife's nephew is coming back home, so we'll give it to him."

Angry words fought for priority on his tongue, but Jonathan managed to keep them caged and simply said, "Do you have any boxes?" He would move his things now instead of making two trips.

"In the alley," was all the man said, "but the furniture is mine."

Jonathan swept past him, glad he wouldn't have to borrow a truck, and let himself out into the small alley full of trash cans and dumpsters. He jogged up the outside metal staircase, trying not to shudder at the thought of Lorne slipping while trying to climb up or down in the icy conditions, and unlocked the door at the top.

Jonathan stared. One glance was all he needed to take in the single room, the camp bed, and the single electric ring next to the sink. And how, even though it was bare, it was nearly as clean as the surgery he sometimes operated in. He put down the box he had carried and knew he wouldn't need another. Two other packed boxes stood to the side. One was a crib that had yet to be built, and the other contained some smaller baby items: a few empty bottles, a sterilizer, some powdered milk, and some diapers.

He opened the drawers in the corner and took out the clothes then gathered up an old laptop and some files. This was Lorne's life, and it had taken him five minutes to pack. Two trips to the BMW were all Jonathan needed, and he took the key back to the man and paid the two months' rent that was owed without a word.

He was pulling into the clinic's parking lot when his phone rang.

"Dr. Owens?" It was Trixie. "I think you'd better come."

Jonathan was running before he realized it. "What's wrong?"

"Mr. Austin's trying to leave."

"What?" Jonathan hung up and ran faster.

He opened Lorne's room door just in time to see him being restrained by an orderly and Trixie arguing with the man. "What the hell are you doing?" And Lorne flinched. Hell, he thought he was talking to him. He looked at the orderly. Jim, he thought he was called. Jonathan didn't see much of him because he worked in the clinic. "Why are you restraining my mate?"

"M-mate?" The man stammered. "I'm sorry. I came to refill the water, and he was just sneaking out. He—"

"Leave," Jonathan ordered, and the man practically ran. Jonathan turned and held out his hand to Lorne who looked in danger of collapsing. "Please?" he asked and waited until Lorne hesitantly clasped his fingers. Jonathan very gently but firmly helped him back into bed then toed off his shoes and climbed in the other side, ignoring the startled gasp from Lorne. Trixie nodded and carefully closed the door behind her as she left. He couldn't pull Lorne close without making it uncomfortable for him, so he eased him forward the same way he had in the bath all those months ago and got in behind him. Lorne tried to hold himself stiffly away from him, but Jonathan just rubbed his shoulders until Lorne relaxed back then he wrapped his arms around him cradling his baby bump.

"I am so very sorry, sweetheart," Jonathan said. "I knew what Gregory was going to say, but I chickened out of telling you, and it was cruel. I should have given you some warning."

Lorne didn't reply for a long moment. "I knew there was something very wrong," he said. "But male omegas never have multiple births, so it never occurred to me."

"I'm sorry I didn't explain before."

'It's not your fault," Lorne said generously. "I knew there was something bad when everyone tried to stop me bonding with them."

Jonathan frowned. "What do you mean?"

"The technician never offered to let me see the screen. She never asked if I wanted to know if I was having a boy—" Lorne's voice broke.

"And none of us have offered to let you hear the heartbeat," Jonathan finished in utter dismay. Lorne was right. They had all done that. Possibly not even consciously, except for the technician whose hands were tied. They had hoped to save Lorne further anguish, and it might have worked if this was the first clinic visit. Mothers were only ever offered this procedure much earlier, certainly less than twelve weeks, but Lorne had carried these babies for six months. He had already bonded, and what they were doing was simply cruel. He was pregnant *now*. He had three very alive babies *now*.

And not even giving him a chance to say hello to them wouldn't make saying goodbye any easier.

Jonathan kissed him on the back of his head and eased him forward so he could get out. "I'll be right back," he promised and nearly ran to the imaging suite where they had the mobile ultrasound. He gathered what he needed and pushed it back. He met Trixie just coming out of another room, and she smiled when she saw what he was doing. "I'll make sure you're not disturbed," she murmured.

Lorne was just wiping his face with tissues when he came back in. "What's that?"

"It's a mobile ultrasound. I think it's about time you met your babies. *Our* babies," he corrected, and it was worth every second to see Lorne's face light up. He should have done this earlier.

He helped Lorne lie down and pulled down the sweats he had gotten dressed in. Then he squirted gel on the wand and clicked on the machine. "I haven't done this in a while," he said and felt a twinge of excitement. He wasn't as good as the technician, but he wanted this to just be them. Lorne could have as many other scans as he wished, but he so wanted to be here for the first time Lorne saw them. He angled the screen so they could both see. "Look." He pointed to what was the biggest bump and turned the sound up. The rapid beats of three hearts filled the room, and Lorne's fingers found Jonathan's arm and held on. "That's the girl." He didn't say the biggest because it was obvious, just pointed out heads and arms. Chuckled when it looked like the girl was kicking one of her brothers and explained how the pouch was different from a female uterus because Lorne seemed fascinated.

"Do you know you don't have an umbilical cord?" Jonathan asked and turned off the machine eventually. He wiped the gel off Lorne and helped him get comfy. Lorne nodded.

"Yes. I've spent the last twelve weeks reading as much as I could."

"When did you find out?" Jonathan came and perched on the bed and took Lorne's hand.

"It was Annabel really."

And Jonathan's ears pricked up. "Is she the one with the omega son called—"

"Matthew," Lorne confirmed.

"Matthew was Bo's witness when he married Gabe. I can't believe you've been so close all this time, and I couldn't find you." Then he had another thought. "What have you done for money?"

"The alpha gave me some cash which lasted for the first couple of months, and he paid for the room."

"And what were you going to do?" He didn't tell Lorne his alpha had *stopped* paying for the room.

Lorne blushed. "I write children's stories. I've actually self-published them, and it's paid my bills for the last few weeks."

Jonathan remembered the files and the laptop.

"Obviously, I wouldn't carry on—"

Jonathan squeezed his hand. "You do exactly what you like. I have a smaller room on the ground floor I can turn into your office." He didn't add he could put a playpen in there because that was very unlikely, and for some unknown reason, the words he'd just said to Lorne ran around in his brain.

You don't have an umbilical cord. And it gave him a ridiculous, incredible idea.

"Anyway, I met Annabel when one of her children ran out in the road right in front of me, and I just managed to grab his arm before a car came. We talked and met a few times then I started getting sick. She knew I was a retired omega, and it was her who urged me to take the test, but she thinks it's my old alpha's baby. She doesn't know about you."

Jonathan focused back on Lorne and just caught the last of what he said. He dropped another kiss on his head. "She'll be thrilled."

"If—if none of them live, you won't need to be saddled with me."

"Whoa," Jonathan stopped him. "Look, I know this is unusual, even for a mating contract, but let's not go down that road just yet." He took a chance. "I'm too busy enjoying having you back in my arms."

Lorne stilled then glanced up at him shyly. "Really?"

Jonathan nodded. "I could never get that night out of my head, and you never answered my question. Why were you gone when I came back upstairs?"

Lorne flushed. "Busted," he muttered, and Jonathan grinned. "Because you were too nice," he whispered.

"Nice?" Jonathan repeated.

"You have to understand. I thought I would always live with them. Mistress told me so many times they were only prevented from a formal arrangement because she's an attorney, and the law tied their hands."

"But the only other formal arrangement is marriage, and as they were already married, it would have been impossible."

Lorne nodded. "And I was stupid enough never to question it. I just believed them."

"And you thought that might happen twice?" Jonathan was beginning to understand. Lorne shrugged, but it might have as well have been a yes. "And I guess the situation you're in now isn't giving you any confidence."

Jonathan considered his next words before he said them. "We could always get married."

Lorne smiled. "That is sweet of you to offer, but divorce is as easy, and while for some it gives them the security they need, it isn't what I want."

"What do you want?"

Lorne shook his head. "Trust. Safety. Three babies," he whispered.

And that was at the crux of everything. Lorne wasn't inept. He was creative and prepared to fight for his babies. He had just faced one problem after another until he needed help.

But that didn't mean Jonathan specifically. He had no doubt Lorne only viewed Jonathan as a means to an end. He was effectively being forced into a corner and was only with him because of the babies. Because he had no choice. And he, of all people, knew omegas were a lot more independent than most people gave them credit for, sometimes when you least expected it.

Lorne yawned and hid it behind his hand. "Why am I sleeping so much?" He looked suspiciously at Jonathan.

"I admit to giving you something earlier when you were so distressed, but that's the only time and really should be the last. Everything in your blood stream goes to the babies." Lorne nodded. "I think it's your body's way of needing to recharge. Don't forget your body is essentially feeding four of you and has been overworked for some time." Jonathan moved and stood up. "Think of it as giving your body a vacation and let me do the heavy lifting for a while."

Lorne took Jonathan's hand, it was the first time he had done so, and gazed at him. "Are you sure?"

Jonathan touched his cheek and watched Lorne's expression soften. His reaction thrilled Jonathan. It was clear Lorne loved being touched, and Jonathan loved touching him. "I need to go home and get a shower and some clothes, but I will be back."

Lorne smiled, and Jonathan couldn't have stopped the kiss if his life depended on it. His lips met Lorne's and rather than the short sweet sign of affection he'd intended, Lorne moaned in the back of his throat, and the sound went straight to Jonathan's groin. He cupped the back of Lorne's head with his hand and threaded his fingers through the silky blond strands of his hair. He lazily explored Lorne's mouth with his tongue and licked and nipped gently at his bottom lip.

"Oh," Lorne gasped when he drew back. Jonathan rested their foreheads together for a minute and tried to ignore the throbbing in his pants. He needed a minute. He couldn't walk outside like this.

"Do these doors lock?" Lorne whispered, and another wave of heat moved down his body.

"I wish," he replied fervently and stood up. Lorne's gaze immediately slid to his pants, and Jonathan groaned.

"I need to walk out of here," he begged, and Lorne snickered.

"Think of the grossest thing you ever saw as a junior doctor," Lorne advised.

Jonathan took a few breaths. "I will be back soon. Trixie will send for me the second"—he put a buzzer in Lorne's hands—"you need me, and I will be back before the shift change so you won't meet anyone new without me being there."

"I don't expect you to spend every minute with me," Lorne said shyly.

"Why?" Jonathan asked, but he didn't wait for the answer.

Jonathan dialed Gregory's cell as soon as he left.

"I'm so sorry, my boy." Gregory answered immediately. "I feel I left you—"

"He doesn't have an umbilical cord," Jonathan interrupted excitedly.

"And you're thinking?" Gregory asked immediately.

"Direct blood transfusion to the fetus."

Gregory fired off rapid questions, and by the time Jonathan was leaving the parking lot for the second time that day, Gregory had agreed to visit and consult tomorrow. It was risky. It was impossible with a female in this manner and had never been tried before, but this was a unique situation. And Jonathan was going to discuss it with Lorne when he got back.

The only awkward thing was the arterial specialist Gregory worked with and knew he would want to be involved. But surely it was past time for her to still be upset. It had been months since they had parted ways.

But no more hiding behind anyone. From now on, he would tell Lorne everything to do with the babies, good and bad. He just hoped like hell he might have a little bit of good to tell him this time.

Jonathan drove straight home because he needed a talk with his nan. Another one. He signaled to turn off the highway about twenty miles north of the clinic and pulled up the pot hole filled lane leading to the large house. He wouldn't care if it had been a family heirloom or something; Jonathan hated the house and had sworn the day he left at eighteen he would never return. His mother and father had bought it shortly before they'd gone on their last archaeology dig, and his nan had moved in after they died. He'd moved back because he'd had no choice when his neighbor had called and told him his nan was basically living in one room because the house was impossible, and Jonathan, much to his shame, realized running from other things had made him distance himself from her. He was appalled and had immediately resigned and was on his way home the next day. He'd done as many repairs as he could, but they were all temporary until they sold it. But it was like pulling teeth as his nan herself would say.

He pulled up and got out his keys, but Nana met him at the door before he got there. He grinned and wrapped his arms around the five feet nothing lady who had been his whole family for a long time.

"I was just dusting in the library, and I saw your car. Come in, and I'll put the kettle on."

Jonathan followed her through the drafty hallway, taking in the stone floor which contributed to the problem of warming the house, along with the antiquated wood burning stove in the enormous kitchen which was supposed to heat the whole house but didn't. He'd had a call yesterday from the engineers who were supposed to be rerouting some of the heating to tell him his nan had vetoed all their suggestions, saying they were a waste because Jonathan was selling. Except he couldn't sell until he knew she was settled. He knew she would be expecting the daily battle to live somewhere else, but he forestalled her.

"I need help."

Her eyes lit up immediately, and he went on to explain who Lorne was and the problems he was facing.

"Well, it sounds like you know what you're doing," Nana said approvingly. "Not sure what I can do."

"Be there for him," Jonathan begged. "He has no one, no family who are interested, and I can't be with him all day. If we can do this—and it's a big if—it means he can't get out of bed for at least four weeks. He absolutely has to stay in the hospital, and while I can be there at night—"

"You have a job to do," Nana agreed.

Jonathan told her about the orderly Trixie had been kind, but she didn't work there seven days a week, and some of the other nurses might not be as sympathetic. There was still a lot of bigotry against omegas; after all, they had been treated like second class citizens for years.

Jonathan was a hundred percent sincere in wanting his gran to spend time with Lorne. He might have an ulterior motive, but he'd tackle that another day.

For now, he needed the two most important people in his life together. And he hoped they might just be what each other needed.

SIX

LORNE DOZED on and off some more and eventually needed the bathroom again. He wasn't so stupid he would attempt it on his own, so even though he hated doing so, he rang the call bell. A new nurse came in a few moments later. She peered down the end of her nose at him, and Lorne squirmed.

"I'm sorry I need the bathroom."

"Well, it's there," she said and turned on her heel and left.

Lorne gaped. He was used to some people's attitudes, but Jonathan had been very strict in his instructions that he wasn't allowed to get out of bed on his own. Although, he didn't see what harm it could do, so he pushed back the sheet. He'd barely eased his legs out of bed when his room door opened again, and Jonathan stood there.

"What are you doing?"

"I—" Lorne froze.

Jonathan's eyes narrowed. "Please tell me you weren't getting out of bed on your own." Lorne pushed the buzzer away. It was still flashing because the nurse hadn't turned it off, and she must have realized that because the door flew open again, and she stormed in.

"Mr. Austin—" Then she shut up when she saw Jonathan. "Dr. Owens," she started. "I was just—"

"Ignoring my instructions?" Jonathan said mildly and turned the call bell off. She bustled over. "I was—"

"It's fine," Jonathan cut her off again. "I'm here. We won't need you for the rest of the evening."

"But—" she looked flabbergasted.

"I can manage to help my omega," Jonathan said in a clipped voice, and she left.

"Are all the nurses scared of you?" Lorne asked as Jonathan helped him to the bathroom and ordered him not to move when he was finished.

Jonathan came back in when he heard the toilet flush and watched Lorne wash his hands then brush his teeth again. "Some of them deserve it," Jonathan said wryly and took his arm to guide him back to bed which two orderlies were making fresh. The young man on the left seemed completely starstruck and squeaked in alarm when Jonathan thanked him. The older woman paused when they were both done and smiled at Lorne. "My name's Maggie."

"Lorne." Lorne immediately replied, and she beamed.

"And that's Cal." The young man smiled shyly. "I'm on all night, so you want anything, you just press your buzzer." She looked at Jonathan. "And you won't be disturbed unless you need anything, Dr. Owens."

Jonathan grinned. "Perfect."

She smiled again and followed the young man out.

"Have you eaten?" Lorne asked.

Jonathan nodded. "With my nan, which is what I wanted to talk to you about. I called the hospital, but they said you were asleep, so I didn't think you would mind. It meant I was a little later though."

"It's fine," Lorne assured him.

Jonathan toed his shoes off and sat on the bed. Lorne noticed he'd changed his dress pants for some comfy looking jeans that hugged his hips, and his mouth watered a little.

"I have two things to tell you. First, I have an idea about the babies."

Lorne tilted his head to listen. Jonathan sounded excited, but like he was trying not to seem so.

"You don't have an umbilical cord because male omegas have a pouch that is secured to the lining of the stomach and fed by a complicated network of blood vessels."

"What does that have to do with an umbilical cord?"

"Because, in females, the cord is responsible for nurturing the baby. In males, you have a direct blood supply which is why there is such a greater risk of bleeding." Lorne nodded. He knew the last bit. "Your current arterial system is just not big enough to supply three babies and I'm questioning whether something could be set up similar to a system of 'cleaning blood' they used years ago. The blood used to be passed through a machine to take out things that people with damaged organs couldn't do without assistance."

"Do you mean like the old fashioned dialysis machines?"

"Yes!" Jonathan's eyes widened.

"My mistress had a lot of old legal books. There used to be an awful selection system way back when organ transplants were necessary before artificial ones were perfected. It sometimes had to go to court for so many reasons."

"And you were interested?"

"I love reading. I'll be honest, most of her law books were incredibly boring, but sometimes I would hear her talking about a case and I was interested enough to go look it up." He lowered his head and picked at an invisible thread on the sheet. "Especially omega rights."

Jonathan nodded. "I can see that, but that's a battle for a different day. I need to see if I can do this first."

"You think you might be able to replicate something similar to feed the babies?"

Jonathan chewed his bottom lip. "I honestly don't know. Gregory is coming back in the morning, and he wants us to consult someone else he knows who specializes in vascular systems. I promised I would tell you everything from today onwards, and I'm sorry I'm not being very clear, but—"

"I get it," Lorne said softly. He knew it was a long shot. "Thank you for trying."

Jonathan smiled and brushed a kiss on his lips.

"You said two things?"

Jonathan looked blankly at him then grinned. "Yeah, I need your help."

"Anything," Lorne immediately responded, and Jonathan shook his head.

"Let me explain before you agree," he cautioned, but his eyes twinkled. "My nan is seventy-five as I told you. I'm selling the out-of-date mausoleum my parents bought. I want her to move in with me to a new house, but she says she will be in the way. I even offered her a new apartment."

"But that's for old people," Lorne joked.

"So I wondered if you'd mind if she kept you company? I know she's lonely, and if we manage the procedure, you're talking a minimum of three weeks, hopefully longer, where you won't even be able to get out of bed. I was hoping she could visit. I have a room upstairs she could even sleep in if she'd agree." He smiled at Lorne. "It's not like I'll be using it." Lorne's toes curled. He intended on staying every night with him?

"Of course," Lorne assured him, and Jonathan yawned.

"Sorry," he said from behind his hand. "Three a.m. delivery that lasted four hours."

"Then why don't you get comfy?" Lorne invited, and Jonathan sent him a steamy look.

"I'm just going to use the bathroom then." Lorne nodded. He was lucky the hospital beds were so big. It wasn't how he was planning on having their first proper night together if you didn't include the one when they met. Jonathan was back from the bathroom in no time. He changed his jeans for shorts. Lorne was rubbing his bump absently when he came back, and Jonathan immediately zeroed on it.

"What's wrong?"

"Nothing," Lorne said and took his hand and flattened it over his belly.

"Gymnast." Jonathan pronounced.

"Or a doctor?"

Jonathan nodded. "Or a scientist. Or a politician. Or an—"

"Omega," Lorne whispered and held his breath. Jonathan nodded and skimmed his hand under his baby bump.

"It doesn't matter. No child of ours will ever be forced into a mating contract." Jonathan sounded quite fierce, and Lorne melted a little more.

Jonathan smoothed his hand along the underside of Lorne's belly, and Lorne hissed.

"What is it?"

"Nothing." Lorne caught his arm as he was bending down to look. Jonathan simply arched an eyebrow, and Lorne let go and hid his face behind his hands.

"What is it, sweetheart?" Jonathan asked gently.

"Stretch marks," Lorne wailed in exasperation. He'd tried so hard, but the good cream was quite expensive, and he had one underneath that was quite sore. He felt so ugly sometimes. He closed his eyes as tears pricked them. He was so selfish, getting upset over ridiculous things like that.

"Hey," Jonathan lowered his hands. "I have just the thing." He fished about in Lorne's cabinet until he brought out a tube of cream. "We keep this in every room. I've been told it's really good." He popped the cap. "Lie back." He looked at Lorne's sweats. "You'd be comfier with them off. Can I?"

Lorne swallowed but agreed, and in no time, he was lying on the pillows with his bump uncovered again. Jonathan pulled the sheet up to his shorts so Lorne wouldn't get cold. He even warmed the cream in his fingers before he smoothed it on.

Except it didn't quite have the soothing effect he had perhaps intended because after a few minutes where Lorne simply floated under Jonathan's administrations, he became hard. And, of course, Jonathan noticed, and his hand kept brushing nearer and nearer his cock. "We can't," Lorne gasped out.

"Well, I'm not sure what you mean, and obviously, there's going to be no penetration, but endorphins are just what the doctor ordered." He slid his hand below the waistband of Lorne's shorts. "And I prescribe lots of them."

"I feel like I should make some joke here about your dispensing methods, but I'm afraid you'll stop," Lorne squeaked out as Jonathan wrapped his hand, still slick with cream, around Lorne's cock.

"You talk a lot," Jonathan murmured and bent to silence him. Lorne returned every kiss as enthusiastically as it was offered until his head spun. A glorious ache filled his balls, and he felt them draw up.

"I'm—"

"Good," Jonathan soothed and met his lips again with his own and swallowed whatever words Lorne was going to say. He certainly didn't remember what they were.

THE NEXT MORNING, Lorne was woken with a kiss and a cup of herbal tea to take his pills with. He felt better now his body wasn't fighting the pregnancy. Jonathan was already dressed when he woke and introduced him to William, a new nurse. William's huge grin was as big as the rest of him, and he was very friendly, so they were soon chatting away. William came from a large family and confided he had nine older sisters. He joked his dad had insisted his mom kept going until they had a boy. What startled Lorne was that both his mom and their omega had had birthed the babies, and they were all just one big happy family.

Lorne wasn't sure he could cope with that, but he guessed it was much better than a lot of arrangements he had seen.

Including his old one.

An hour later, Lorne was just flicking through a magazine William had found when the door opened and what looked like a dozen doctors walked in. Okay, so that might be a slight exaggeration, but there were a lot of them. Jonathan immediately came to the bed, followed by Professor Denholm "Good morning, my boy." The professor smiled, and all the other white coats hushed expectantly. He sat down on the chair at the side of Lorne. "Now, I know Jonathan has briefly explained what we are going to try and do, but we need to do some tests this morning to see if the idea isn't as mad as I first thought."

"It's theoretically possible," a female murmured. "Depending on if we can get to the full arterial system without disturbing the pouch."

"This is Dr. Anne Coulson, our vascular specialist." Jonathan told Lorne, but she didn't so much as look at Lorne, and Lorne, while not being bothered in the least, could tell Jonathan wasn't pleased she hadn't acknowledged him.

He didn't think anyone else could tell though, and he glanced at Jonathan while he was listening to the professor and Dr. Coulson discuss the intricacies of making sure the return venous system was intact, and how really it was only because the pouch was the exact opposite of a female's uterus that it had any hope of working at all. Lorne let all the technicalities wash over him because while he'd been fascinated with the possibility, the medical jargon was a little confusing.

Jonathan argued a point then, seemingly without being conscious of it, he slipped his hand into Lorne's. Lorne was thrilled because it had been an automatic gesture. He loved when Jonathan touched him. Lord, he'd loved it last night especially. The slight tightening of Jonathan's fingers focused Lorne back on the conversation.

"It increases the viability of the whole procedure. Surely one healthy fetus, or two, is better than losing all three."

Lorne's skin went cold when he realized what she was suggesting, and he glanced up at Dr. Coulson. "I thought this was instead of doing that." His words were quiet, but everyone in the room hushed immediately.

"Insisting on trying to save them all might be as good as condemning them all," Dr. Coulson snapped. Jonathan bristled, but Lorne beat him to it. This was his fight.

"I understand the scientific arguments," Lorne said, trying to stay calm, "but you cannot expect me to choose to end one of their lives."

"On that we are in agreement," she said. "I would make that choice during surgery, but you can't end the life of something that cannot exist independently."

"That they cannot *live* independently from me is a separate issue." It was one thing doing the procedure when he was in his early weeks, and he understood how that made sense, but not now. He would never presume to make that decision for someone else—he certainly wouldn't judge anyone else for making that decision—and he resented being forced into it. Even the kicks and tiny movements were taking on a personality.

Jonathan stood up and thanked the doctors for being there and focused on Lorne

taking his other hand. He barely noticed the other doctors leaving, but suddenly, there was just them. "Okay, this is what has to happen."

Lorne opened his mouth, but Jonathan quirked an eyebrow, and he closed it.

"We are scheduling the procedure for tomorrow morning. Our intention is to save all three babies, but there is a chance we won't be able to because of arterial placement. If that decision has to be made, I will make it while the surgery is actually happening, and you won't know anything about it because I'm giving you a general anesthetic."

Tears sprang to Lorne's eyes. He shook his head mutely.

"It's the only way, and you're going to have to trust me. If I can save all three, I promise I will. If I can't, then you will have to trust me to make the decision for you." He slid his arm around Lorne's shoulders and peppered kisses on his head which was pressed to his chest.

"But, as of right this moment anyway, you are confined to bed. We cannot take the risk the pouch will degenerate anymore before tomorrow, because no alternate blood supply will work if the pouch itself fails."

"I thought you did well not to lose your temper with her," Lorne commented, still trying to wrap his head around everything.

Jonathan stiffened, and Lorne wondered if he'd said the wrong thing. "How did you know?"

"Because your lips go straight, and you hold yourself incredibly still."

Jonathan looked at him, bemused. "I didn't even realize." He took a breath. "But Dr. Coulson is one of the best arterial specialists there is and wants a position at a new research facility. Gregory's recommendation would go a long way to her getting it even though she thinks we're all crazy for attempting this in the first place."

"Because it's so risky?"

Jonathan flushed, and Lorne understood immediately. "Because I'm an omega, and she can't understand why you would go to all this trouble in the first place." To be honest, part of Lorne agreed. The other point of a limited mating contract was no one wanted to be stuck with an omega who was of no use to anyone.

He'd once read a book about when male omegas were successfully enabled to get pregnant. The same story Professor Denholm considered "romantic." The original scientist *had* lost his wife and baby during childbirth, but because he was over a certain age and females were so scarce, they wouldn't allow him to marry or take a mate when there was such a strict selection process involved. It was his work to find an alternative that started the whole thing, and omegas—particularly male ones—had once been treasured and adored by a threatened population.

Not so much now.

"Hey." He felt Jonathan's finger tilt his chin up, and he looked at him. "Don't go there. I hate it when you question your worth."

"How did—"

"Because you're not the only person who notices things, and you don't have to worry because you're not on your own anymore." Jonathan kissed him. And it wasn't gentle. He didn't glance his warm lips over Lorne's in an effort to tease him. He just took the kiss; it was as demanding as it was definitive. Stamped with possession and everything alpha. Lorne was his. He was telling him so in the best way he knew how, and Lorne raised his arms to get as close as he could with three babies in between them and simply hung on.

It didn't last for long though because Jonathan had other patients to see. But before he left, Jonathan bent to pick up a box from the floor Lorne hadn't noticed and handed it to him. Lorne stared open-mouthed because he could see the name on it and knew what it was. "You bought me a new laptop?"

Jonathan grinned and wheeled the table over that was big enough to fit over his bump. He placed the old one on his bed along with some memory sticks so he could transfer everything, along with his paper files from his room. "Everything else is still in the trunk of my car I'm afraid, but we have plenty of time to sort everything out."

Lorne lifted his face automatically for the kiss he knew was coming and stilled in shock just as Jonathan's lips met his. Already? They had already gotten to the point where he could interpret and even anticipate Jonathan's actions? Jonathan left before he could articulate his thanks properly with a admonition he wasn't to overtire himself and to use the buzzer for anything he needed.

Jonathan would be back to check on him, and his nan would be by to visit later.

Another hour and Lorne had transferred his files and left his new laptop to charge properly. William had come in and cleared the boxes away, refreshed his water, and replaced his nutritional supplement with a very slow running saline drip.

"I thought it was stopping today?" Lorne asked. When William started fiddling with his IV, he thought he was removing it.

"They will leave it in for surgery just to be on the safe side."

"Oh, okay." That made sense.

"Plus, you won't be getting anything to drink in the morning, and heaven help us all if you should get dehydrated."

William said it with a twinkle in his eye, so Lorne knew he was teasing him about Jonathan's overprotectiveness. There was a knock on the door just as William was finishing, and William opened it to a small elderly woman. Lorne knew immediately who she was and where Jonathan had gotten his gray eyes from. William fussed, getting her a comfier chair and offering her a tea or a coffee which Lorne was glad of because he was suddenly tongue-tied. He knew this lady was all Jonathan's family and very important to him, and he was suddenly scared of making a bad impression. In fact, William had only just whipped away the bottle he had to pee in before she arrived.

William put her coffee down then suddenly he was gone, and the room seemed very quiet. The lady picked up her purse and fished about in it, pulling out a small bottle. Eyeing Lorne, she put a finger to her lips in a shushing motion then poured some of the contents into her coffee.

Lorne couldn't help the huge grin from spreading across his face, even when she noticed. "Well, you can't have any, so I'll just have to have enough for both of us."

And that was that. She insisted Lorne called her Nana then they talked babies. All babies, not even just the ones he was expecting. Nana had even brought her knitting, and she patiently showed Lorne how to cast on for a cute, yellow cardigan he admired.

They were both giggling over Nana's pregnancy tales, including when she'd had thrown up in her very expensive purse because there was no other container and they were stuck in the car, when the door opened and Jonathan came in.

He sighed dramatically. "Nana, did it ever occur to you I was sending a car? The driver called me in a panic when you weren't at home."

"Jonathan, I am completely capable of using a telephone and getting my own cab," she scolded but tilted her face for a kiss on her cheek. Jonathan took in the coffee, the knitting, and probably the huge smile on Lorne's face and relaxed visibly. Lorne held his hand out, swallowing the lump down in his throat. Jonathan had worried. How did he ever deserve such a kind man?

"I was just explaining everything to Nana," Lorne said as Jonathan clasped his fingers. "And I'm so glad she'll be there when we bring them home." He'd confessed he was terrified at the thought of looking after more than one baby at a time, and Nana had countered dryly that surely it was what he had done before. She had obviously thought Lorne was just trying to butter her up because Jonathan wanted it, but Lorne actually realized it was true, and over a few tears and another coffee—decaf for him—Lorne admitted he wasn't as confident this time around. Nana had patted his hand and told him he hadn't didn't need to worry about a thing.

Jonathan couldn't stay long because he had an emergency patient as well as an afternoon clinic. "I can't believe how incredibly lucky I am," Lorne whispered without thinking before he remembered he wasn't alone. He'd already told Nana what had led to him being there.

Nana took his hand. "I think it's Jonathan that's lucky," she offered. "He's been alone a long time."

Lorne turned to her. He hadn't liked to ask, but he assumed his parents had died.

"My son and daughter-in-law met in college. They were both archaeologists, and while they wanted a child, they were completely uninterested in anything involving his care as a baby. Having said that, even as a young child, Jonathan was intelligent and articulate, and they enjoyed their time with one another."

"Did he have an omega?"

Nana smiled. "Yes. And Declan was amazing. He was everything Jonathan needed, so much so that he never missed his mom or dad when they went on all their overseas trips. Anyway, they were in charge of excavating the ruins of a city called London that was completely decimated in the great wars, and there was a landslide. Their whole party was buried."

"Oh my goodness. I am so sorry." Lorne reached for her hand.

"My son was killed instantly, but Jonathan's mom was alive for two days before they found her in the rubble. Jonathan flew straight over there with Declan and me, but she had a massive heart attack just as they freed her, and there was nothing they could do."

Nana sighed. "It was awful, but it was what happened shortly afterward that was ten times worse. You have to understand Jonathan wasn't close to his parents. I'm sure they loved each other in their own way, but they were never affectionate to him, and he never missed it because of Declan. Declan was there for every scraped knee, every school prize, and even when the boy Jonathan wanted to take to a school dance decided to go with a girl."

"What happened?" Lorne knew there had to be something.

"Jonathan had his fifteenth birthday three weeks after his mom and dad died."

"Which meant the contract ended, but surely that wouldn't have mattered."

"You would think, yes. I mean my son was diligent. He even had it spelled out that their own deaths didn't negate the contract. That nothing did, failing Jonathan's own death, I suppose. But as you know, it is the law that all omega contracts finish on the youngest child's fifteenth birthday."

Lorne nodded.

"Jonathan was at school that day, and I had gone back to the city. I didn't actually live with them at that point. Jonathan walked in the door to find Declan with his bags packed. He was sorry, but he had money that Jonathan's mom and dad had left him in their will, and he was set to start a cruise that weekend."

Lorne gaped. "He left Jonathan to go on a cruise?"

Nana swallowed. "And Jonathan was heartbroken. I didn't know until I got a call from school the next day to report Jonathan hadn't turned up for an important exam. I tried to call and got no reply, so I drove straight down there. He was in the bathroom throwing up with the world's worst hangover because he had raided his dad's liquor cabinet the night before." Nana clutched his hand. "He told me the world assumed he was now a grown up, so he'd decided to become one."

Nana shook her head.

"That's awful," Lorne said, his heart aching for Jonathan as a boy.

"Yes, and it changed him. He was always the same with me, but he gradually distanced himself from all his friends and concentrated on school. He worked so hard I was frightened he would have a breakdown, but he remained completely driven. I moved in immediately."

"Did he ever see Declan again?"

Nana shook her head. "No. We got a few postcards, the odd email. He wrote to me full of the news he had been offered a job taking care of some politician's son, but I never replied. I still hadn't forgiven him."

"I don't blame you." And Lorne wondered what that meant for them. Jonathan had said he didn't want an omega but had then done a complete about turn when he had discovered Lorne was pregnant. He'd even offered to marry him. Was that because he really wanted Lorne to be his husband, or was what he actually wanted was to make sure his own children didn't lose their omega like he had done?

And suddenly, he was very much afraid it wasn't about him at all, but what he was. And he honestly wondered if he would ever be seen for anything more than that.

SEVEN

LORNE HAD BARELY SLEPT. He'd managed to stay reasonably
still because he wanted Jonathan to get some sleep, but his surgery
this morning was completely terrifying him. He knew Jonathan
would try his hardest, but what about the other doctor? What if she
didn't try as hard because she didn't think an omega was worth
saving? And she was the one with the task of managing the blood
supply which was the whole crux of the matter.

"Lorne?"

Lorne shifted so he was on his back and turned to look at
Jonathan. He hadn't been able to settle at first because of his little
athletes and had tried to distance himself from Jonathan so he
wouldn't keep him awake. That hadn't really worked. Then a sleepy
Jonathan had ordered him to get on whatever side he was most
comfortable with and had snuggled into his back and thrown a
protective arm across them all. He had dozed for a while, but his
brain simply wouldn't turn off to let him sleep.

"You shouldn't sleep on your back."

Lorne turned a little on his side. He knew the weight of the
babies pressed on a vein that took the blood to his heart. He'd read

that. He'd read everything he could, but nothing had been written about omega multiple births because they didn't happen. "Is this better doctor?"

And Jonathan smiled, reaching over for a kiss. "You should have woken me. I bet you've lain and worried all night."

"And I think, under the circumstances, I'd worry even more if you were tired. I need all of your concentration this morning," he teased.

"Gregory is in charge of the procedure. I'm not allowed, because you're my mate." He frowned. "Which reminds me, I have our mating contract to read through whenever you're ready."

Lorne nodded. He tried to take a few steady breaths, but the risks of this morning seemed to loom larger the more he tried to calm down. Jonathan rubbed a thumb across Lorne's jaw. "You'll be fine."

Lorne swallowed. "I don't care about me." He put a hand protectively across his bump. None of them were moving, and panic slammed into him. "Jonathan, they're not moving. What if somethings wrong? Can you?" But Jonathan had already slid out of bed and unhooked the stethoscope from the equipment arranged above his bed. He smiled reassuringly and put the end onto Lorne's belly when Lorne yanked his T-shirt up.

He nodded then took it out of his ears and solemnly arranged it in Lorne's. "Listen," he instructed, and the heartbeats thumped very reassuringly in Lorne's ears.

"Is that all of them. Are you sure?"

"Yes. They're fine." Then, for no good reason, Lorne burst into tears. Jonathan tutted and bent down; scooped Lorne up, covers and all; and sat down in the chair with him, cradling him and dropping kisses on every patch of skin he could reach. "I promise I will do my very best."

"I-I know," Lorne wailed and cried some more. "I know you will," he added after another moment and turned his face into Jonathan, not caring in the least if his T-shirt became wet.

He heard the door open but didn't look.

"It's okay, Trixie, give us a few minutes."

Lorne's sobs died away under the gentle kisses and the strong arms cradling him. "I'm sorry," he whispered after a few minutes.

Jonathan kissed him again. "You have absolutely nothing to be sorry about. Now, I need to check if Roger is okay with my patients then I have to make sure everything is ready. Trixie will be here with you when I'm not, but all you have to do is say the word, and I will be back." Jonathan slid forward with him and eased him out of the chair, helping him back to the bed. "Professor Denholm will be here at nine. You're first, so you have less time to worry."

Which was fine in theory, but even though Trixie was very kind and calming, she sighed when she checked his blood pressure. "You're getting worked up." She pressed the call button. Another nurse came in who Lorne also liked, and Trixie handed his chart to her and told her to take it to Dr. Owens.

Sure enough, Jonathan arrived, accompanied by Professor Denholm. He shook his head but smiled at Lorne and immediately took his hand while Trixie took his blood pressure again.

"Hmmm, I think we'd better get him a little relaxed. I don't want any last-minute problems," Professor Denholm remarked.

Lorne blinked a little. Suddenly, an image appeared in his head of him lying naked while Jonathan dispensed his pheromones, making him flush.

"And take his temperature," the professor added to Trixie. "He looks warm." Lorne wanted to die, especially when he caught the wink he sent to Jonathan. Gregory patted his head. "I'll see you in a little while."

The second nurse came back into the room with a small dish containing a syringe, needle, and a small vial. Lorne swallowed. "Is it safe?"

"It's safer than your raised blood pressure," Jonathan assured him and quickly injected it into the line going into the back of his hand from the IV.

"I'm sorry," Lorne said because he knew Jonathan wouldn't do anything to hurt them. He rubbed his gritty eyes. "I'm just—"

"I know." Jonathan toed off his shoes and simply got in bed behind Lorne. Trixie was still coming in and out, but she never said a word, so Lorne didn't either.

"You never told me if you had any ideas for names."

Lorne relaxed back and let Jonathan take his weight. He had a few ideas, but he had tried not to think about it recently. "What's your Nana's name?"

"Hope."

Lorne smiled. "Perfect. And I'd like her middle name to be Annabel because she was nice to me."

"What about boys?"

"The only one that means anything to me is Nicholas."

Jonathan nodded. "I like Rowan, but I don't have a definite preference." He kissed Lorne on the head, and Lorne took a deep breath. He relaxed some more and yawned. "You can shut your eyes you know. I won't leave you."

"Mmm," Lorne replied because he was already drifting. Two orderlies arrived with a gurney, and Lorne tried to force his eyes open. He must have nodded off. Jonathan eased himself out from behind him and bent down to give him another kiss.

"I have to go get changed and scrubbed up. Trixie will stay with you the entire time I'm not there." Lorne smiled lazily. He was fine. Jonathan could go do whatever he needed. He really had no idea why he was worried. He yawned again.

He opened his eyes, and Jonathan—dressed in scrubs—was squeezing his hand. "Is it done?" Lorne mumbled.

"No, sweetheart. I just wanted to let you know they're going to put you to sleep now, and I will be right with you the whole time and when you wake up."

Lorne opened his eyes with effort. "Promise?"

Jonathan nodded, and the technician asked Lorne to confirm his name but all Lorne said was "Jonathan's omega." He heard Jonathan

chuckle and whisper "not just" before he yawned again, and everything became way too fuzzy for anymore talking.

AN EXCRUCIATINGLY LONG four hours later, Jonathan sat with his
head in his hands by the side of Lorne's bed. It was done, and
Jonathan never wanted to go through that ever again.

"Did we lose them all?"

Jonathan raised his head at the terrified whisper and clasped
Lorne's hand. "No, sweetheart. It was touch and go there for a few
minutes because the blood work was complicated. We were worried
for Hope, but she's fine."

Lorne's face beamed. "She is?"

"And so is Nicholas." Jonathan brought Lorne's hand to his lips
and kissed Lorne's fingers. "And so is Rowan, or whatever we're
gonna call him."

Lorne's pulse jumped. "Really?"

The curtain moved. "You told our boy the good news?" Professor
Denholm asked, coming to stand next to Jonathan. He beamed down
at him.

"Just," Jonathan confirmed.

"Good, well, I want you to stay in bed for as long as we can
stretch this out. Get these babies to twenty-eight weeks at least. I'd
like them there as long as possible, but I don't think that's going to
work, simply because the pouch is already stretching to full capac-
ity. It doesn't have the same flexibility as a female uterus, I'm
afraid."

"I understand."

"I'd love to say you're completely out of the woods, but at least
they have a better chance now."

"Thank you," Lorne said solemnly.

"You are welcome, my boy," the professor said as he left.

"Now, what I need you to do is rest." Jonathan brushed the hair away from Lorne's eyes. "Shut your eyes, and we'll explain everything when you wake up."

Jonathan stayed while Lorne had been transferred and was resting. He had a patient to see and was extremely relieved when Nana arrived.

JONATHAN LET himself in Lorne's room sometime later to find Lorne asleep and Nana knitting. She looked up as he walked in and gathered her knitting together, putting her finger across her lips. He followed her outside.

"I was thinking, Jonathan."

"Oh no," he teased and grinned at the disapproving look he got.

"Do you think we should make any attempt to contact Lorne's family?"

Jonathan shook his head. "They abandoned him at the omega facility before he was even eighteen. I don't think so."

Nana smiled. "I don't mean that one."

"His ex-Alpha?" Jonathan wanted to ask if she was insane, but he managed to reign himself in.

"No, I mean the children. Specifically, Nicholas because he's an adult. I just thought, if they missed him, it would be nice to find out rather than Lorne himself reaching out and getting rejected."

Jonathan considered it for a few seconds. "That's actually not a bad idea. Because if they don't care, he never needs to know."

"And if they do, it would be a nice thing, especially as the next however many weeks are going to be incredibly frustrating for someone who is used to hard work."

"He could write."

"Yes, but I mean physical hard work."

Jonathan agreed. He knew depression could be an issue. After all, that was one of the reasons he'd involved his nan. Nana smiled and announced she was going to go home, get a bath, and come back tomorrow.

Jonathan let himself back into Lorne's room and smiled when Lorne immediately opened his eyes. "How are you feeling?" Before Lorne could answer, he offered him some water which Lorne sipped.

"Relieved," Lorne admitted. "I know," he added when Jonathan opened his mouth. "I know nothing's certain yet." He looked at the IV bags he was hooked up to, particularly the red one.

"Our other big challenge, apart from keeping the pouch viable, is infection. Your incision area will be kept covered and only handled sterilely."

Lorne reached out, and Jonathan clasped his hands. "I need you to stop worrying. Starting tomorrow, there's going to be a physiotherapist called Amber visiting daily who will be helping you stay as healthy as possible while you are stuck in bed. You can sit out in a chair, but to be honest, I think you will have more room to stretch in bed. Just no moving at all without someone here."

"Yes, doctor," Lorne teased.

Jonathan cupped his cheek. "I like it when you follow orders."

Lorne sucked in a tiny breath, and his pupils grew bigger. Jonathan bent down, completely unable to stop the kiss after that reaction. He groaned as their lips met and stopped after a moment with some difficulty.

THREE DAYS LATER, Jonathan was happy Lorne had gotten into some sort of routine. He had physio every morning, his dressing checked, and a scan to make sure everything was in place. In the afternoon, he was allowed visitors. Nana came every day, and he was immensely grateful they got on so well.

Jonathan was standing in his office, tapping his cell phone with one finger, and debating whether to call the number he had tracked down. Nicholas Carmichael was an attorney and seemed to be a successful one. He had spoken to his friend Gabe's sister Emma who had nothing but good things to say about him. What he didn't understand was, if he was so good, why he'd let Lorne disappear, and why he'd let his father treat him like a piece of unwanted baggage.

Still, he trusted Gabe, and Gabe trusted Emma. He dialed the number.

"Nicholas Carmichael."

"Mr. Carmichael, this is Dr. Jonathan Owens from the Omega clinic in Granley, Northern Sector."

There was a silence.

"Is there someone needing my services?"

"No. We have a Lorne Austin here. He's—"

"Lorne?" Jonathan heard a chair scrape as Nicholas obviously stood up. "He's sick?"

"My mate has had some treatment, but I would rather not—"

"Your *mate*?" Jonathan interrupted again, incredulity in his voice.

Jonathan paused, wondering why he'd felt the need to stipulate that. Technically, Lorne hadn't signed anything. "Yes." Jonathan took a breath. "I will be extremely blunt, Mr. Carmichael. Lorne has spoken of you and your sisters with a good deal of fondness, but he was devastated to be practically evicted from your—"

"*What* did you say?"

Jonathan hesitated. "Your father made Lorne leave the day your younger sisters turned fifteen." This time the pause was caused by the number of expletives Nicholas used.

"I had no idea. My father told us Lorne had chosen to leave when his contract ended, and he wanted to go quietly so as not to spoil the twins' birthday. I knew that was completely ridiculous," Nicholas carried on without pausing. "The Lorne I knew—even if he'd decided to go on the vacation he so thoroughly deserved—would never have left without telling us where he was going. I've been trying to find him for months, but it's impossible."

Jonathan smiled. He knew how Nicholas felt.

"Is he okay?" The worry was obvious in Nicholas's voice.

"He's being well looked after," Jonathan prevaricated because he wasn't going to tell Nicholas anything without talking to Lorne.

"Can I see him?"

Jonathan agreed immediately as that was what he had been hoping for. Nicholas had to be in court tomorrow, and much as he would love to be there straight away, he couldn't miss it. But the day after was Saturday, and he could finish early and hoped to be here for Sunday.

EIGHT

LORNE LOOKED up at the soft knock on the door, and William put his head around. "You ready for visitors?"

Lorne was completely overjoyed to see Annabel. She beamed and stood to the side so he could see who else was with her. The young man smiled shyly and said hello, but Lorne was too entranced by the bundle in his arms to even say hello back. "Oh," he breathed out the word.

"This is Bo, and his daughter Sammy. Gabe has a cold, so he thought he'd better not come."

"Congratulations," Lorne said as they came near. He shook himself and managed to remember his manners. "I'm sorry. And congrats on getting married." These were obviously Jonathan's friends.

"Thank you," Bo said, dimpling, "and here you go."

Lorne had his hands extended as soon as he realized what Bo was going to do, and then he had an armful of delicious baby. He swallowed and gazed at the gorgeous blue eyes that were blinking up at him, the soft wispy brown hair, and the perfect little pink lips. "Oh my goodness, you are stunning."

Bo giggled. "I knew I was going to like you."

"How old is she?"

"Seven months. She's had the sniffles, and obviously Gabe caught it, now he's got the dreaded man-flu." Bo rolled his eyes. Nana came back in, and within a few seconds, Annabel and Nana were discussing quilting which Annabel was interested in, leaving Lorne and Bo to talk uninterrupted. Bo got a bottle out when Sammy started fussing. "You would think when they did all the science stuff, they'd have made us able to feed," Bo griped good-naturedly.

Lorne nodded. "Wouldn't that be wonderful?"

Bo shivered. "Sore nipples. She's teething."

"Maybe," Lorne allowed and went to hand her over to her daddy.

"Would you like to feed her?"

Lorne looked up in excitement. "Yes, please."

"Good," Bo said and handed everything over. "I may take a nap," he joked.

"Help yourself," Lorne replied, completely in awe at how much she reminded him of Sophie.

"Of course, you've done this before." Bo observed how easily Lorne handled her.

"I have but fifteen years ago." He smiled, remembering.

They chatted while Sammy finished her bottle and went to sleep. Nan and Annabel went to the canteen, promising to bring something back for Bo, and Bo told Lorne all about her birth. And how he was convinced Gabe had been his very own Christmas miracle.

"Or maybe you both were his?" Lorne pointed out, and Bo laughed.

"You've certainly performed a miracle around here. Gabe was stunned when Jonathan told him he was getting mated. You've succeeded where not even his fiancée did."

There was an odd little silence after that where Lorne absorbed what Bo had let slip, and Bo looked horror stricken. "Gabe's going to kill me."

Lorne forced a wide smile. "It's okay. I'm not surprised. Good looking alpha and all that."

Bo gazed at him, the apology stark on his face.

"It's really fine."

Bo chewed his lip thoughtfully. "I guess it doesn't matter though. The important thing is he's yours now." They said goodbye when Annabel and Nana came back with Jonathan. He chuckled when he saw Bo and immediately went to admire Sammy. Annabel offered to take Nana home and promised to come back in two days but told them to call if there was anything she could do. Jonathan left as well to answer a summons about another patient.

Fiancée. Jonathan had been going to get married. He obviously wasn't married. Did that mean she'd left him? And what did that mean for them? People kept telling him Jonathan had sworn to never have an omega. Jonathan had even told him that himself. Jonathan had been attentive and kind, but the more he learned, the more he was convinced that when Jonathan came back down to earth from all the baby excitement, he was going to regret their mating. He'd spent the last fifteen years in a loveless mating contract. It would kill him to do it again.

Lorne was surprised a little later when he saw Dr. Coulson walk into his room. It was the first time he had seen her after his surgery, and to be honest, he didn't think she was still here. The technician was just finishing his ultrasound as she had been late today and commenting that she thought Nicholas was catching up to his sister in size.

Dr. Coulson peered at the monitor and asked a couple of questions, all the time not even acknowledging Lorne, but then she surprised him by picking his chart up and staying in the room after the technician had wheeled the machine away.

The silence was a little awkward. Lorne took a breath. "Jonathan told me you were hoping to work in a new research facility."

She looked up as if surprised he had spoken to her. "Yes, but that will depend on Jonathan I guess."

Lorne was puzzled. What did it have to do with Jonathan? But he didn't get the chance to ask as the older nurse that had been a little short with him walked into the room and said Dr. Coulson was needed in the clinic. She nodded and handed her the chart, asking for some blood to be drawn from Lorne and naming a barrage of tests the nurse understood but he didn't. "What are the tests for?"

Dr. Coulson glanced at him. "I've asked for Estriol, Inhibin, and AFP protein," she rattled off in a bored tone.

But Lorne was sick of being treated like he didn't matter. "And they are?"

"Basically, we order those tests to establish whether there is a risk of birth defect or spine abnormality. Most of the original chromosomal defects—the original purpose of some of these tests—have now been eliminated, but obviously, you are a special case."

"You're testing for birth defects?" Lorne felt sick.

"Well, oxygen depletion carries risk."

"Oxygen depletion?" Lorne tried to keep the panic out of his voice.

"Of course," Dr. Coulson replied in the same monotone voice. "It was explained to you that the pouch and the arterial system that supports it was never designed to house more than one fetus, and that the damage may have already been done."

"Anne!"

They both turned to see Jonathan standing in the doorway, glaring at her.

She shrugged and put the chart back. "You know my opinion on this." Without another word, she swept out of the room.

Lorne slid his hands protectively over his bump.

The damage may have already been done. "What did she mean?" But it was a stupid question. He knew what she meant.

Jonathan sat down on the bed and took Lorne's freezing hands. He always seemed to be cold. "All the tests we are doing used to be regular second trimester ones. We still routinely test for this in all male omega pregnancies and some female. You know there was a slim chance the babies were not getting the nutrition they need—"

"But she said oxygen."

Jonathan sighed but nodded. "Because the blood carries oxygen. Technically, she is correct."

"You promised no secrets." He was sick of finding this sort of thing out from other people.

"Okay then." Jonathan nodded. "You might get an embolism from bed rest which could give you a heart attack or go to the brain and cause a blockage or a bleed which would likely kill you."

Lorne stuttered. *"W-what?"*

"The pills that we give you every morning could get swapped with another patient's and cause an allergic reaction leading to anaphylactic shock."

Lorne frowned. That seemed a little unlikely even to him.

"Masked assassins fighting for omega rights might blow up the clinic."

Lorne arched an eyebrow.

Jonathan leaned forward. His lips were an inch away from Lorne's. "Nana might trip up as she comes in and stab you with her knitting needle."

His lips twitched. "I may stab *you* with her knitting needle."

Jonathan clutched his chest with both hands over his heart. "I'm mortally wounded."

"Oh no," Lorne joined in. "What can I possibly do to save you?"

Jonathan gulped noisily. "K-Kiss me. It's the only way."

So Lorne did. Enthusiastically. No one could ever accuse him of not knowing how to deliver mouth to mouth resuscitation in an emergency.

LORNE MUST HAVE DOZED AGAIN—BIG surprise—because he opened his eyes to the sound of his door being flung back. It was the nurse he didn't particularly care for, and she smiled distractedly then let her eyes skim over the room. Then she hurried to the bathroom and peered in. Lorne watched in fascination and kept quiet because of what he could see behind the large chair next to his bed.

"Is everything all right?"

She tutted. "An alpha is having some awful trouble with his omega. Kind enough to bring him here himself because the boy is too temperamental to be trusted to look after himself, and now he's disappeared. The poor man's beside himself with worry."

"Well if anyone comes in here, I'll press the call bell immediately," Lorne lied.

The nurse shot him a distracted smile and left. Lorne counted to five. "I think she's gone," he whispered and glanced down to the chair.

The slim young man with the bandaged arm who was crouched behind it cautiously got to his feet. "Th-thank you," he said so quietly if Lorne was any further away, he wouldn't have heard him. Lorne patted the bed.

"Are you okay?"

The young man's eyes filled with tears, and he shook his head. Lorne reached out his hand immediately. The poor child didn't look much older than Sophie and Suzanna.

He didn't take Lorne's hand but stepped a little closer staring down at Lorne. "You're pregnant."

Lorne smiled immediately, guessing this may be an omega. "Yes, and as incredible as it seems, I'm expecting triplets."

The man's mouth opened in surprise. "I didn't know that was even possible."

"It isn't usually. Which is why I'm in here and confined to bed." Lorne put his hand out again. "My name's Lorne."

"Shay," the man said in a hushed voice and took Lorne's hand this time.

Lorne patted the bed, and Shay sat down. "Are you going to tell me why you're running from your alpha?"

Shay paled. "How did you know?"

Lorne ran an assessing eye over Shay. Shadows under his eyes. Bruising on his temple. He dropped his gaze and saw more bruising on his wrists. "You need help."

Shay hesitated. "No one can help me."

"My alpha could." He didn't know how, but he was sure Jonathan would. Then the door opened, and Lorne had a second to gape in surprise at the man who was standing there with Jonathan when the nurse from before followed them in, and Shay was seen.

"Alpha," she called, and the room was suddenly very full of a large man Lorne had never seen before, and two men that looked like security guards.

"Shay!" The large man said, sounding relieved, but from the way Shay paled, Lorne guessed this was his alpha. Without missing a beat, Jonathan turned to the alpha. "I need to do a few more routine tests we missed today. Perhaps you could come back tomorrow or Monday?"

The alpha seemed to grit his teeth, his grip on Shay very firm. "Is that really necessary?"

"I'll be as quick as I can," Jonathan promised. He smiled at Shay. "I'll see you Monday."

Shay glanced back at Lorne with such despair, it was all Lorne could do to stay in bed, but Jonathan came up to him and took his hand, squeezing it in a warning manner, so Lorne just smiled back as Shay left.

"I can't do anything to give that bastard one reason for him not to come."

"What's the problem?"

And Lorne focused on Nicholas. Nicholas glanced at the closed door.

"The problem is my hands are tied," Jonathan heaved out frustratedly.

"Nicholas?" Lorne said in awe, and Nicholas turned, a smile breaking out on his face. He strode over to the bed and bent down, wrapping both arms around Lorne and clutching him tight for a few seconds.

"I didn't know. The step-bitch insisted you wanted to leave, and I couldn't find you. Sophie and Suzanna were heartbroken." He stepped back and nodded to Jonathan. "I still wouldn't know where you were if Jonathan hadn't tracked me down."

Lorne put a hand to his mouth when his throat got really tight.

Nicholas perched on the bed. "I can't believe you never contacted me. You had to know I was out of my mind with worry." And he gazed at Lorne, enunciating very clearly. "If this is what you want and you are happy, then I am happy, but I just want you to know you aren't without friends. You aren't without family." He glanced at Jonathan. "I checked, and there are no mating papers filed. If you need a mate, and obviously my father is useless, then I would be honored."

Lorne opened his mouth, but Jonathan butted in. "There are no papers filed because we've been a bit busy, but Emma Redding whom I understand you know has drawn them up."

Lorne squeezed his hand in understanding. "Nicholas, the babies aren't your father's. They're Jonathan's."

Nicholas seemed to notice Lorne's huge belly for perhaps the first time, and his eyes rounded. *"Babies?"*

"Yes, triplets. Which is why I look so much further along than I am, and why I'm here on bed rest."

JONATHAN UNDERSTOOD. He really did. He'd called Nicholas himself.

But.

But what? He was threatened because another alpha was suddenly giving Lorne an alternative? Was he really so insecure? Just because Nicholas had history with Lorne? Just because they were clearly comfortable with each other? Just because Nicholas was a successful younger man who was currently holding Lorne's hand?

"I'm going back to clinic," he offered before he walked out, but he wasn't sure they had even heard him.

Clinic was long. He was just looking at Shay's x-rays and wishing he had an excuse to admit him when Anne came into his office. For once, her face was flushed and she was even smiling. It was rare enough to distract him.

"Jonathan. I wanted to tell you first, but Andover Medical has just offered me a place on their genetic research team."

His eyebrows rose. "Congratulations. Impressive." And it was. While the science behind gender selection had been available for a long time, he knew a lot of people were interested in taking it one step further and looking at parents being able to choose if they wanted an Alpha or not. Currently, Alpha males and females had a seventy-five percent chance of conceiving another alpha. The percentage was greatly reduced in betas which is why, when two betas mated , they were only allowed to have two children by the same archaic laws that controlled omegas.

He was sure there had been some similar law about gender selection in certain areas of the world back before the great wars. Privately, he was sickened by the whole idea. Children should be loved for who they were, not what they were, but he knew Anne was very much in favor.

"We would make a good team."

Jonathan focused quickly. "Team?"

Anne took a step to close the gap between them. Jonathan had to grit his teeth not to step back. "You know they want both of us." She shook her head and waved her hand to encompass the room. "It's almost criminal someone of your ability is stuck in a small local birthing clinic."

Jonathan opened his mouth, but Anne cut him off. "I know you had to rush home because of your grandmother, but we could build her a suite of rooms, and the omega would be very useful to take care of her. Obviously, I wouldn't want children myself, but seeing as how there is a slim chance you may have one—"

"Anne, I'm very flattered, but we agreed to part amicably because we wanted different things. What makes you think things are different now?" He had no intention of marrying the woman, but he was curious.

"Free omega healthcare."

Jonathan's eyes widened.

"If you agree to a five-year contract, they will open a state-of-the-art omega clinic to be run as you see fit. No charge at point of need and no questions asked." Anne smiled, knowing she was dangling a huge carrot. Jonathan had fought for years over the very subject. *Kayden.* He would never forget his name.

He had gravitated into obstetrics because he liked working with Gregory, and it had interested him. He hadn't even been fully qualified the first time he had worked in the ER, and Kayden had been admitted. He had run from his abusive alpha, and terrified and alone, he had managed to hide his pregnancy and even get a job waiting tables. He had been thirty-five weeks pregnant when a cop had found him passed out behind a dumpster and bleeding heavily. His daughter had been stillborn, and he had lasted another two days. His emaciated body could not recover quick enough, even with everything they tried, and his heart had finally given up.

Anne nodded like he had spoken. "I don't need an answer now. You have a few weeks to think about it, but at least promise me you will consider their offer."

"And yours?" he said bluntly. "Is one dependent on the other?"

Anne shrugged. "No. But we worked well together. You have to admit that."

Jonathan sat down heavily after Anne had left. It was true. They had worked well together, and for a long time, he had been happy with her on a personal level as well. In fact, the only thing they ever argued about was omega rights. Anne was completely focused on her career. They had a very small circle of friends, but with both their jobs, they barely had time for a social life. Then Jonathan had decided to specialize in male omega pregnancy, and they had drifted even further apart. They had just decided to part ways when Nana had her accident. Within the space of a few hours, Jonathan's life had completely changed.

He was tempted. A facility offering free health care for omegas would be fabulous, but it was in the eastern sector and miles away. He just wasn't sure he could stomach furthering research to provide what he essentially disagreed with even to get what he really wanted.

But people fell easily from high horses, and the omegas needed him now.

He would have a battle with his nan, and while technically Lorne would have no choice, he hated to even think of that. But Lorne did have a choice. A very successful alpha who seemed to like the idea of being Lorne's mate.

And so did he.

Yes, he could take the babies, but he would never do that to Lorne. Jonathan put his head in his hands. What the hell did he do?

NINE

TEN DAYS PASSED with Jonathan no nearer to making a decision, and no nearer to having the guts to talk to Lorne about it. At least Nicholas had gone back, but the school holidays were approaching, and Nicholas was determined to bring his sisters to see Lorne.

Lorne was excited. Nicholas had arranged for the twins to stay with him for a week while his father and step-mother went on a cruise. It all worked out perfectly, but Jonathan was frightened it would be one more nail in the coffin for him and Lorne.

It started with Trixie. Clinic was three afternoon's per week, and she had asked Jonathan if he would allow the male omegas that came to clinic to visit after with Lorne, and at the same time, Roger broke his ankle. Vivian—another doctor–was on her honeymoon, so Jonathan offered to be on call while she was away. After the first night when Jonathan's pager had gone off seven times, he had reluctantly slept on a cot upstairs so he didn't disturb Lorne. Between Nana, the omegas, Annabel, her mom and family, the line of Lorne's visitors was getting longer. And while Lorne was glowing from all the attention, he needed sleep.

Jonathan disturbing him would do him no good. In fact, after a full week, Jonathan thought he'd maybe had thirty minutes uninterrupted time with his mate.

He was just standing up and stretching after his last patient left when there was a knock on the door, and he opened it to see his nan. He smiled tiredly and kissed her proffered cheek.

"Nicholas has been back."

Jonathan was surprised. He hadn't known although Lorne would be happy to see him.

"He's bringing the girls tomorrow."

Jonathan nodded. "Lorne will be happy."

"Jonathan, has Lorne signed the mating contract?"

"I—" He hadn't mentioned it again to Lorne. He didn't want to push him. "I hate backing him into a corner when he's under so much pressure."

She reached out and cupped his face, exactly the same as she had done when he was a little boy. "Why don't you arrange some cover and do something nice for your omega?"

Jonathan thought. Vivian, one of the other doctors was back from vacation. Maybe she wouldn't mind covering for a few hours even if she technically wasn't due to start work until tomorrow. He smiled. "What do you suggest?"

"Date night," Nana said promptly.

Jonathan chuckled. He couldn't take him anywhere. They couldn't share a meal. What else could he do? Just then another knock on the door heralded Amber coming in to drop off some notes. Jonathan thanked her. "How's Lorne?" Amber did physiotherapy with him every morning.

"Sore," she winced.

His eyes flew up.

"Can I be blunt?" she asked worriedly. "He can't stand up. He's getting terrible indigestion every time he tries to lie down and sitting is becoming very painful."

Jonathan skimmed through her notes. His skin was intact, but Amber was worried. There were only so many positions he could get any rest in. And hell, Amber had started noting this three days ago, and Jonathan had been so busy looking after every other patient he hadn't paid enough attention to the most important one to him. He tapped his finger on the phone and dialed Trixie who was hopefully still here. She came in barely a few seconds later. "Trixie do you still have any contact with that medical equipment specialist?"

Trixie blushed. "We're getting engaged in the summer."

Jonathan smiled widely. "I need his phone number."

LORNE GLANCED at him with tired eyes when Jonathan let himself in his room an hour later, but his smile was just as genuine. Jonathan had already showered in the changing rooms and arranged for them not to be disturbed. He wanted to talk to Lorne but didn't know where to start.

In bed was as good a place as any though, and he immediately slid in next to him. "Did Shay come to clinic?" Lorne immediately asked and tried to move onto his side a little.

"No, but there's one tomorrow." Jonathan brushed a kiss deliberately on Lorne's smiling lips. "I'm sorry I've hardly seen you all week."

"You had patients—"

"You're my patient," Jonathan interrupted, and Lorne's smile fell. The silence grew and Jonathan could have kicked himself. "Amber says you're getting sore." Which wasn't what he meant to say at all. The trouble was he didn't know what to say. Of course, Lorne was more than his patient, but just calling him an omega seemed worse.

"I'm okay."

Jonathan put his finger under Lorne's chin and tilted it slightly. "I want you to be more than okay." He took a breath. "And you are more than my patient." He smoothed Lorne's cheek with his thumb, and Lorne's eyes deepened. He loved that reaction. It was honest. No matter what they were saying, or not saying, to each other, Lorne couldn't hide his body's reaction.

"Get undressed my omega," Jonathan murmured, and Lorne's eyes darkened until the violet was nearing black. His breath hitched just before Jonathan took Lorne's mouth with his own. Jonathan sucked and licked. Nipping at Lorne's bottom lip and grazing his teeth with his own tongue. Lorne tried to bring his arms around him, but he couldn't get close enough, and Jonathan heard the sigh of frustration. "Turn on your side," he instructed and gently pulled the T-shirt over Lorne's head and the sweatpants down. Each inch of skin he uncovered got a kiss. He paused when he got to Lorne's hips. His bones were sticking out far too much, and his ass was red. Lorne hissed as Jonathan ran his hand over it.

"I have ordered something to help tomorrow." Jonathan nibbled at the back of Lorne's neck. "But this may help until then." He drew a tube of cream out of his pocket and put it down beside him while he undressed.

Lorne smiled lazily. "You take my mind off all my aches and pains."

"Not enough," Jonathan said honestly. He'd left him alone far too much this week, and no excuse was good enough for that. "Close your eyes," he whispered, and Lorne yawned. He warmed the cream in his hands and started on the back of Lorne's neck. Within five minutes, Lorne seemed to have melted into the mattress. Jonathan wasn't convinced he was even awake. He was very gentle on his hips and ass.

"Amber doesn't do that," Lorne murmured. "I think I need a new physio."

Jonathan grinned. "She starts doing that, and you're definitely getting a new physio." He bent and kissed Lorne's shoulder.

"I feel very lazy."

"Good," Jonathan praised him. "You're feeding, nurturing, and keeping safe three babies. It's me that's being lazy compared to all your hard work."

Then he snaked his arm around to Lorne's front. His cock, which was half hard, thickened as it pressed into Lorne's ass. Lorne wriggled and pushed back temptingly. "Stay still," Jonathan almost begged.

"Why?" Lorne asked. He turned his head a little.

Because. Lorne was stuck in bed. Pregnant. Dependent on Jonathan.

Because... Lorne moved again, and all the reasons why he shouldn't seemed to disappear as a wave of heat swept over his groin. Then Lorne moved again, and Jonathan bit his lip.

"I know you can't be inside me," Lorne whispered, "but I so want to give you the same amount of pleasure you've given me." And very carefully, with help from Jonathan, he turned over so they were facing each other. Jonathan squeezed some more cream on his hands and reached under Lorne's baby bump for his cock. Lorne groaned, sighing in pleasure and reached for Jonathan.

At the first touch, Jonathan was nearly seeing stars. "Your hands are so soft," he whispered. Lorne tightened his fingers and slid them over Jonathan's glans. Jonathan made some sound in the back of his throat that didn't quite qualify as speech and immediately sought Lorne's mouth with his own.

They quickly established a rhythm. Harder on the upstroke and softer on the down, and to Jonathan's delight, Lorne found his voice. Shyly at first. Small encouraging noises then whispered pleas to go faster, twist his wrist just so, beg as he thrust his hips, and never stop. Never ever stop.

Jonathan had had sex more times than he could count, and he usually like it both rough and fast. A gallop to the finish line, barely remembering to kiss, not a gentle meandering mapping of another's body and discovering how they tasted. Jonathan was entranced. Wrapped in their own world, promises of mutual pleasure enmeshed with a bone deep need to give to the other.

Lorne's pupils were round and wide. His moist lips parted. Sweet gusts of air puffing against Jonathan's face when he wasn't swallowing them down. Copious precum leaked from them both. Then

Lorne's breath caught, his cock pulsed, and Jonathan was helpless to do anything other than kiss him deeply as cum spurted in his hand. He was so lost in Lorne's taste he barely felt his own release a few seconds later.

He pressed his lips to Lorne's one last time, wishing he could get closer, and smiled as he felt an indignant nudge from Lorne's bump.

Lorne giggled. A carefree happy noise that completely thrilled Jonathan. Reluctantly, he eased out of the bed and cleaned them both up, fetching a warm soapy washcloth for Lorne and making him as comfortable as possible. "Pick a side," he suggested.

Lorne sighed and rolled on his left. "I'm half asleep now."

"Good," Jonathan eased himself behind Lorne. "Promise to tell me the second you get uncomfortable."

A shy nod and barely five minutes later, Lorne was asleep. Jonathan thought he was maybe a few seconds behind.

JONATHAN KNEW Lorne had barely slept after the first few hours. He'd tried everything he could think of short of sedating him, but he didn't dare risk it with the babies. He would rethink if his "surprise" didn't work.

He came out of the bathroom to see Lorne watching him. He looked even more exhausted than yesterday. Lorne glanced at the door as William walked in and smiled. He looked at Jonathan. "How do you want to do this?"

Jonathan pushed the easy chair into the corner. "I'll lift Lorne, and you can make sure all the equipment follows us."

"Where am I going?" Lorne asked.

"We just need you out of the way while we move the bed," William answered cheerfully. Jonathan bent down and carefully lifted Lorne and the top sheet, walking to the armchair and arranging Lorne on his lap. William made sure all his tubes were secure.

Lorne flushed. And yeah, Jonathan could have just settled Lorne down in the chair, but he loved any excuse to have his arms around him. William went back and opened the door and unhitched the second door as well.

The bed was huge. Lorne watched in astonishment as two technicians wheeled the it in and started putting it together.

"A new bed?" Lorne asked.

"It's called wave technology," Jonathan explained. "It constantly changes pressure points minutely while you have to lie in the same place. It simulates nearly constant movement, but I'm assured it's incredibly relaxing."

"But it must have—" Lorne clamped his lips closed.

"Good choice," Jonathan whispered. "I bought it, but the clinic will buy it from me at a discount when you are done with it."

Lorne shook his head in disbelief. "I can't believe you got me a bed."

William giggled. "Better than a ring," he joked.

Only Jonathan heard the slight hiss of breath at his words. And didn't *that* give him something to think about.

An hour later, Lorne was back in bed, and the technician was showing him the different programs. "It's amazing," Lorne said after he had gone, and everyone else cleared out. "Thank you."

Jonathan mentally patted himself on the back, but before he could take another kiss, there was another knock on Lorne's door, and Nicholas popped his head around. "Ready for your birthday present?"

Jonathan whipped his head back to Lorne. *Birthday?* But before he could so much as say a word, there was a huge squeal from the door as two bodies barreled in and launched themselves at Lorne.

The twins. Jonathan stood back and watched as the girls were overjoyed at seeing Lorne.

"Nicholas said we could get you something finally now you're not an omega anymore," the tallest of the two nearly identical girls said and grinned, handing over two large bags packed with gifts.

But he is an omega Jonathan wanted to say. *He's my omega.* And he hadn't even known it was Lorne's birthday.

He should have. It wasn't like his date of birth wasn't clearly marked on every form. Clothes, books, pictures. Lorne laughed in delight as one gift was three teddies. One pink and two blue. And what had Jonathan got him?

He watched as Nicholas hugged Lorne gently.

A stupid damn bed.

Way to go.

TEN

ANOTHER WEEK and the magic twenty-eight was nearly in sight. Apparently, as Jonathan had explained, because the pouch operated slightly differently than a female's uterus, twenty-eight was considered the holy grail. In females, it could be as early as twenty-four. Jonathan had gotten out of bed around three a.m. to see to an emergency patient, and he was absent when the technician came in to do his morning scan. Lorne watched as the screen showed three beating hearts, but even he could see it was getting snug in there. In fact, snug might be a generous term, and the technician had been quieter than usual. Lorne wasn't stupid. He knew the babies would start having serious problems very soon. Stacey—the technician—seemed to hover over a particular area to the left of Hope more than previously.

"What is it?" Lorne couldn't keep silent any longer.

Stacey looked up. "It's a little worse," she admitted. "I'm just going to get Dr. Owens to come and look." She stood up and went to the phone on the wall and sure enough in a few minutes Jonathan came in followed by Anne. Lorne barely took any notice of her though because Jonathan looked awful. Something had obviously upset him, but with an audience, Lorne couldn't ask.

To be honest, he wasn't sure even without an audience he could ask. Ever since the night Jonathan had given him the new bed, he had been a little quieter, less demonstrative. As attentive as always, kind and considerate, but almost as if he was holding something back, distancing himself. Lorne thought there had been something wrong with the babies he wasn't telling him at first, but Professor Denholm had been by two days ago, and he had seemed quite jovial.

Lorne came to the conclusion it must be something wrong with him. They hadn't made love since, but to be honest, he couldn't blame Jonathan for that. By the time Jonathan had finished work for the day, Lorne could barely keep his eyes open.

He would never have guessed how exhausting it was just being in bed.

Jonathan gazed at the screen while Stacey pointed out the area she considered a problem, and Lorne's heart sank as he listened. Anne didn't try and keep anything from him, and for once he was grateful for her no-nonsense honesty even if she wasn't directly speaking to him.

"The pouch is clearly degrading closest to the female fetus," she declared and rattled off some blood test orders to Trixie who was standing next to her. Lorne let the words wash over him and fixed his eyes on Jonathan's hand. Why wasn't it in his? He lifted his gaze and watched as Jonathan stared at the screen, mouth flattened. The small tick in the side of his neck showing his pulse beating a fast rhythm.

Too fast a rhythm, Lorne thought almost dispassionately when his seemed to have slowed almost to a stop.

"I'll leave you to discuss, but really, we need a decision in the next few days." Dr. Coulson left, along with the others, and Lorne was left wondering if he'd missed some of the conversation while he'd been wondering what had happened to Jonathan.

Jonathan finally looked at him, but the defeat in his eyes made him want to cry. "What happened?"

Jonathan looked nonplussed. "We have a decision—"

"No." Lorne shook his head. He knew what decision they were

going to have to make, and he was quite happy to avoid it for another few minutes. "I mean before you came in."

Jonathan's eyes widened, and he stared at the hand Lorne extended. Lorne curled his fingers around Jonathan's and, for a second, reveled in the absolute strength it contained. He pulled a little until Jonathan moved and sat down. "It was an emergency delivery."

Lorne nodded. "What went wrong?"

Jonathan hesitated.

"Tell me," Lorne encouraged. "I'm stronger than I look."

Jonathan's lips tilted, mirroring the tiny smile on Lorne's. "You're one of the strongest people I know."

And suddenly, Lorne knew. The defeat in Jonathan's eyes. The slump in his shoulders. "You lost a baby," he whispered.

He nodded. "It was early. Far too early." He raised his head. "Much earlier than ours."

"Did I know them?" He had been visited by many omegas over the last couple of weeks.

"It was Shay."

Lorne's heart squeezed. "Oh no." Shay would be devastated. "What happened?"

"We don't know," Jonathan nearly growled. "His alpha says he fell on the stairs, and he has a witness—a business colleague—who backs it up. Shay's too distraught to make any sense at the moment, and we've sedated him, but his alpha is making noises about moving him to a private facility tomorrow."

"Can he do that?" Lorne was horrified.

"We've contacted the authorities. We have every right with his unexplained injuries, but until Shay either confirms or denies, my hands are tied."

He'd lost a baby. It would kill Jonathan. "Sit behind me," Lorne whispered. He knew it was Jonathan's favorite place, and much as Lorne wanted to be the protector in this scenario, he knew the alpha in Jonathan needed it more than he did. The thought that Jonathan had been helpless in that situation would be killing every alpha bone in his body.

But more than that.

Jonathan was simply a good guy. He would hurt because Shay was hurting.

Jonathan settled in behind Lorne, and Lorne leaned back. "I love it when you hold me like this. I feel like nothing bad can ever happen."

He heard the resignation tinged with a little irony in Jonathan's voice. "I know what you're doing."

"Good," Lorne said. "So, what do you want to do about ours?"

Jonathan sighed. "You heard. The pouch is degrading to the point it's soon going to be putting Hope's life at risk. We have to make an urgent decision. And when I say urgent, I mean in the next day or so."

"For surgery?"

Jonathan nodded. "Lorne, if there was anything—"

"I know," Lorne interrupted. "I've known we are on borrowed time since the day I came to the clinic." He linked his fingers through Jonathan's and rested their hands on his belly. "They don't have enough room. The thought they might have to be fighting each other for everything they get—"

His throat closed. It was a nightmare. That one child might benefit from the death of another.

Jonathan smoothed his hands over Lorne's bump. "I will do everything I can. I promise."

Lorne tilted his head up. "And I believe you." Jonathan brought his head down for a kiss. For some reason, in the middle of all the awful, it grounded him and made his toes curl.

Jonathan eased out from behind him and went to the phone on the wall. He heard him asking reception to arrange locum cover for all his patients and to put in an urgent call to Professor Denholm.

Jonathan put a rush on the blood tests, and Lorne heaved a huge sigh of relief when they were okay which gave him a good chance of delaying things another few days. Nicholas had brought the girls again, and he was sitting with Lorne while Suzanna and Sophie went to the gift shop.

"Are you happy?"

Lorne focused on Nicholas's earnest expression. "I don't know," he replied honestly. "I think I'm so worried for the babies I don't have the room to feel anything else."

"I've been doing some research," Nicholas admitted and pulled out a file. "I wanted you to have options."

"I don't have any," Lorne patted his hand. "Unmated omegas aren't allowed to keep their babies."

Nicholas sighed. "That's not what I mean."

"I don't think Jonathan will give them up," Lorne said. "And sweet as you are for wanting to protect me, I feel more like your dad than a mate."

Nicholas grinned. "That's because you took care of me better than my parents. You were obsessed with everything I ate after you saved my life."

Lorne rolled his eyes. He never ever wanted to go through that again, even if Nicholas had successfully had the cell replacement therapy to prevent the allergic reaction as soon as the procedure was made available.

Nicholas nudged him. "Karma will come for her."

And Lorne took in Nicholas's implacable expression and guessed it would. He also realized Nicholas hadn't been as oblivious about the incident with the EpiPen as he had thought.

"I feel the same about you to be honest, but..." Nicholas continued in earnest. "I want to know you have a home."

Lorne smiled. "And that's sweet of you, but I have no choice."

"Actually," Nicholas let go and tapped the file with his finger. "You might."

"What do you mean?" Lorne was confused.

"I mean there was a successful case—two actually—in the last twelve months where the babies were granted to another alpha, other than the father."

"*Really?*" But even as he said it, Lorne wasn't sure how he felt. Jonathan had been nothing but kind.

"Yes. The omega wanted to mate another alpha and successfully petitioned for the mating contract to be dissolved because they had proof of abuse from the original alpha. The court granted the dissolution on the condition a new one was signed immediately. The children stayed with the omega."

"But Jonathan hasn't abused me," Lorne protested.

"No," Nicholas admitted. "But technically I could site abandonment, and I know which judges to put a case like this in front of." Nicholas took Lorne's hand. "You're usually a good judge of character. How do you feel about Owens?"

"Like we're both being backed into a corner."

"Mr. Austin?"

Lorne jumped. It was Dr. Coulson, and he'd been so engrossed in what Nicholas was saying he hadn't heard her come in. "I'm afraid your visitor will have to leave as we have some more tests to do."

Lorne suppressed a sigh, but Nicholas got up and left, promising he would be back at the weekend. Dr. Coulson didn't say so much as one word to him, but then Jonathan came back and he couldn't help the tentative smile, even with what Nicholas had told him. He was so confused. She turned to Jonathan as he came in.

"Did you get the chance to speak to Shay Nichols? His alpha is insisting on taking him."

Jonathan stilled. "No. I haven't seen him."

"Well, his alpha had just got here when I left."

Jonathan shot an agonized look at Lorne. "Go," Lorne urged Jonathan. It was important.

Jonathan smiled and thumbed his cheek. "I promise I won't be long then we have to talk." He smiled as a nurse bustled in with some fresh water. Lorne agreed. They really needed to talk. He had to find out what Jonathan wanted. The trouble was he wasn't sure which answer he wanted to hear. They'd known each other a matter of weeks. Lorne had known Nicholas for sixteen years. He wasn't sure that even the promise of something else was worth that big a gamble.

ANNE FOLLOWED Jonathan outside of Lorne's room and spoke before he had chance to. "Nurse O'Donnell?" She called to William. "Is Shay Nicholls's alpha still here?"

William frowned. "Shay was discharged around twenty minutes ago."

"Damn," Jonathan said softly and turned back to Lorne's room.

"Jonathan?" Anne put a hand on his arm. "Can you spare me five minutes?"

Jonathan nodded. He did owe her for Lorne. It had been her vascular work that had gotten the babies the three extra weeks they had so desperately needed. And he had decided he wasn't going to take the job. He wasn't leaving, and he owed it to Anne to tell her now he had made that decision. He knew full well his nan wouldn't agree to go, and he had another idea he wanted to speak to Lorne about. He followed Anne into the small office.

"Jonathan, have you signed a mating contract with Lorne?"

Jonathan bit off an instant retort to tell her it was none of her business, but to be fair, she was still waiting on a decision about the job.

"And before you ask this has nothing to do with the research post."

Sure, it didn't. "About that. I've actually decided—"

"Because you're going to lose him."

Which immediately shut Jonathan up. "What makes you think that?" His heart beat, hard.

"Because he's going to mate the attorney. Nicholas Carmichael."

"Since when?" Jonathan almost laughed. "There's no way he will give the babies up."

"According to Carmichael, he won't have to. I walked in as they were just discussing it. He was telling Lorne he'd successfully gotten two mating contracts dissolved and can argue technical desertion against you. The fact that you've now known about Lorne and the babies for three weeks and you still haven't offered him a contract apparently is another nail in your coffin."

Jonathan sat down heavily.

"Carmichael works the system, Jonathan. He has a lot of points in his favor, not least the fact that Lorne knows and trusts him."

Which Jonathan could do nothing about. "I'll get the contract signed." Why had he left it so damn long? Lorne would think he wasn't interested when he'd just been trying to give him time.

Anne put a hand on his arm. "You need an attorney. My brother Charles would be able to advise you."

Jonathan frowned. "I don't need an attorney; I need to sit down and talk through everything with Lorne."

"While he's scared witless for his babies' lives?" She arched a brow. "We both know my strength with patients is generally when they happen to be unconscious," she said dryly, and Jonathan almost laughed, or he would have if sick panic wasn't clawing at his insides. "But even I know you need to find out exactly where you stand first. If you go in and push a contract on him, it may backfire, and according to Carmichael himself, the contracts were dissolved so they made no difference."

"So I do nothing?" Jonathan was aghast.

She shook her head. "No, of course not. I think he's looking for trust and dependability and who can give him that. I also think your best advantage over Carmichael is your age. Carmichael could meet someone tomorrow and marry. His wife or husband may not like Lorne or the fact he already has children." She took a step towards him. "Now this I will freely admit is in my favor, and yes, I am totally using this to my advantage, but Lorne knows me. If we were to marry,

I'm sure it will take no convincing at all that I would never want children of my own. He seems quite fond of your grandmother. All that equates to a family dynamic that won't change. Carmichael's could alter at any time. I believe above all else he wants stability for his children and himself. He doesn't want the chance of being thrown out in fifteen years."

Jonathan searched Anne's face. She was being self-serving, but honest. She totally and one hundred percent admitted that. Was that easier to trust?

"I'm not attracted to you," Jonathan said bluntly. Not anymore. In fact, he wasn't sure if it was simply the lack of opportunity to meet someone else that had thrown them together in the first place.

Anne nodded. "I figured that out, and the other point I should make is that was half the reason why we were crap in bed."

Jonathan's eyebrows rose. She was being direct.

"The other reason is that I simply don't find you sexually attractive either. But again, being honest, I'm more interested in you helping me with my career. Everything else we can work around."

Jonathan was stunned. He didn't ever think Anne had been that direct with him when they were dating. He took a couple of breaths and tried to think.

"Think about it, and I will talk to you later," she said and left the office.

Was she right? Would it work? He hadn't considered Nicholas a proper threat because he knew Lorne wouldn't give up the babies, but if Lorne didn't have to, it put everything in a new light.

ELEVEN

ANOTHER DAY. Another blood test. Lorne tried to suppress the sigh when he saw William with the needles. "You're a vampire aren't you?" William's eyes twinkled in shared humor. Jonathan had just left to collect his nan. He said he wanted to talk to them both about something, and he seemed to be quite excited. Dr. Coulson came back in as William left and studied the scans from this morning. He moved and managed to knock the buzzer off the bed which she picked up without saying a word and put it on his bedside table.

"Thank you."

Dr. Coulson turned to gaze at him almost as if she had forgotten he was there. "Has Jonathan explained what will happen if we are forced to perform surgery in the next day or so?"

Lorne wanted to say yes, but he couldn't. He knew Professor Denholm was coming to see him later, and that was one of the things they were going to talk about. Jonathan said he wanted Lorne to know all his options, depending on the condition of the babies when they were delivered.

"They will certainly be moved of course."

"Moved?" Lorne repeated in alarm. "Why?"

"Because for them to have any chance of survival, they will need a neonatal ICU, and obviously there isn't one here."

"Does that mean I will have to move?"

"Possibly," she agreed. "It makes sense for the surgery to be performed there, but as I understand, the problem is a free bed for you. We only have three of these facilities in the entire Northern Sector, and they all seem to be struggling to accommodate three infants. I think that's one of the things Jonathan is trying to arrange this morning."

Which was scary but made sense.

"It will likely be that you are transferred for surgery, and then the babies remain there, and you are moved to wherever they have a bed, or discharged."

Lorne's heart started thumping almost painfully. "I won't be with them?"

She shook her head. "They will be in for weeks, perhaps months. You will be discharged as soon as you are eating and drinking which will be forty-eight hours at the most. All parents of premature babies have to go through exactly the same thing."

Lorne had nothing to say. He didn't doubt for one second everything she told him was technically correct, but he couldn't help feeling she was a cold bitch. He hoped once this was over with he would never see her again.

"The nursing staff have years of experience with this and will show you when and how you will be able to talk to them and eventually touch them."

Cold washed over Lorne. He couldn't touch them?

"And how to enable you to eventually bond. All the risks to watch out for, especially once you get them home."

Was she doing it on purpose? And if so for what reason? Or was this the bare facts without them being dressed up by Jonathan to make them easier to hear?

He looked down, wishing she would leave, and, after a few seconds, was relieved to hear the door close. He looked for the buzzer because he was starting to feel uncomfortable like he needed to pee. She had put it on his locker, but it was awkward to reach around all the cards and the flowers his new friends kept sending him. He stretched his arm out and hung onto the bed but he still couldn't quite reach. He leaned over and stretched again.

"What are you *doing*?" Jonathan barked from the doorway which made Lorne jump and a cramp shot through his side. He tutted and rushed over. "What do you need?"

"To pee."

Jonathan went to get his bottle from the bathroom, and Lorne felt under the sheet to pull his shorts down. He wasn't sure he didn't want to call Nicholas and ask for his advice, even if he didn't know why. Nicholas wasn't a doctor. Maybe he just needed a familiar face. Trixie had said he could use the phone at any time and had shown him how to dial an outside line.

He grabbed hold of his shorts and froze in complete horror and embarrassment at the wet patch where he had obviously peed a little.

Jonathan came back with the bottle and put his hand out to pull at the sheet clearly intending to help.

"No," Lorne gasped out louder than he intended. He couldn't. He couldn't let Jonathan see.

"What is it?" Jonathan's voice was so gentle. It just wasn't fair. "Let me help."

"No, please," Lorne closed his eyes in shame. "Please just go."

"Go?" Jonathan repeated. Bewilderment coloring the word. "Sweetheart, what's wrong?"

Lorne raise tear-stained eyes. "I-I'm wet," he almost wailed.

Jonathan's expression softened, and he went to pull the sheet again, but Lorne jerked it up. Another sharp pain speared his side, and he gasped.

Worry registered in Jonathan's eyes, and he yanked back the sheet. "What—" He took one look at Lorne and whirled around to the phone dialing the emergency number. Within a second, he was back and pushing Lorne back to lie down, but it was too late because

Lorne had seen. His pants weren't wet because he'd peed. They were wet because of the bloodstain which seemed to be getting larger.

"Lie back." But Lorne could barely hear through the fog that seemed to have surrounded him. He didn't understand the urgent words. He barely heard the door opening, and the sound of feet running. He knew his bed was moving. He stared up as lights on the ceiling flashed past. He knew someone was holding his hand and running at the side of him as they barged into another room. The last thing he knew was the soft kiss on his cheek and the mask laid over his nose and mouth.

It was here. The moment he had been dreading for weeks. The moment when he would go to sleep and wake up a dad.

Or not.

TWELVE

LORNE DID his best to open his eyes, but it seemed like they were glued shut. He knew he needed to, but he was warm and so sleepy. And Jonathan was holding his hand. He knew it was his alpha. Jonathan's scent was immediately recognizable in the way it wrapped him up, like his strong arms. Cradling him.

Almost—

Lorne's eyes shot open, and his breath stalled in complete and utter panic.

"Hush, breathe," Jonathan soothed, and Lorne heard a machine bleep noisily. He moistened his lips.

"How—" he daren't ask.

"They're alive," Jonathan understood immediately. "And they have the best team of doctors and nurses looking after them. You did so well." Lorne felt a kiss on his cheek. The machine bleeped again.

"Doctor," a voice said warningly, and Lorne heard Jonathan issue instructions from what seemed far away. He felt a thumb smooth his cheek and someone touch his hand to keep it still. Coldness ran up his veins.

"Shut your eyes," Jonathan cajoled. "I'm going to take care of everything."

Lorne wasn't sure anyone could do that, but he did as he was told.

THE NEXT TIME HE WOKE, his belly hurt, and he winced a little.

"Hey," he felt a thumb brush the side of his face and opened his eyes to look at Jonathan's gray ones. He gave Lorne what looked like the buzzer he had in his room. "Press this when you hurt." He gently pushed Lorne's thumb down on the button. "It gives you a dose of painkillers when you need a little extra."

Lorne bit his lip, and to his complete frustration, his eyes filled again.

Jonathan wiped them immediately. "This is what I know so far. All three are alive and in the neonatal intensive care unit at Danbergh General—"

"What?" Lorne squeaked out.

"We don't have the level of expertise they need here," Jonathan explained. "And I know being in a separate hospital from them is awful, but it's about the same distance from my house as the clinic so it won't be any further to visit." He smiled. "We didn't talk about this, and that is my fault, but they may be in there for a few weeks." Lorne gazed at him in horror. Dr. Coulson had been right. Did that mean she was right about everything?

Jonathan nodded. "They need to put on enough weight to be able to regulate their own body temperature."

He heard the words, but it was as if he didn't understand them. Earlier bitter words were running around his head.

"Look." Jonathan smiled and handed him three photographs. Lorne stared down at the babies. "Ohh." He traced the outline of the tiny forms with his finger.

"That's Hope." Jonathan pointed to the baby on the left. "Rowan and Nicholas." He pointed out the other two. "Hope is three pounds, two ounces. Nicholas is three pounds even and Rowan is two pounds eight ounces."

Lorne sucked in a worried breath. "That's tiny."

Jonathan nodded. "They are all on ventilators because at this age, their lungs aren't developed well enough to breathe on their own." Lorne swallowed his tears down. He knew they were in the best place, but he ached to see them.

Jonathan stood up. "You're going to be taken back to your room now. I'm going to check for an update and meet you there." He squeezed his hand. "I know it's so incredibly hard but try not to worry. I promise as soon as I know anything, you will."

It seemed all Lorne could do was sleep, and before he knew it, it was the next morning, and he *hurt*. Physically, mentally. He felt like he'd climbed the highest mountain he could find on his knees, clinging on by his fingernails, and when he got to the top, there wasn't even a view. He felt empty even though every time he had opened his eyes, his alpha had been there.

Nana came in, and he couldn't even dredge up a smile for her. "Lorne?" She took his hand worriedly. "Are you in pain?"

He was, but he didn't know how to describe how he felt. Like there was a cloud pressing down on him. She tutted. "What have you had to eat?"

He shook his head. Jonathan had tried earlier. He remembered that. "I'm not hungry." Her eyes narrowed.

"Jonathan's on the phone to the hospital now."

Lorne's heart jumped. What if they weren't okay? He closed his eyes ready to shut out the awful news. He couldn't bear to be told they were sick.

After a while, he must have fallen asleep again because the next time he woke up, Jonathan was sitting next to him and Nana had gone.

"They're stable," Jonathan shared immediately.

Stable? What was that? What did that even mean; he wasn't sure he wanted to know?

"They have a nurse called Aimee caring for them. She will still be on duty when we get there."

"What?" Lorne's heart started thumping.

"I'm having you transferred. You need to be with *them*, not nearly thirty miles away. And I managed to get the professor to pull some strings. Hey." Jonathan wiped under his eyes. "What are you crying for?"

Lorne shook his head. "What if they don't know I love them?" But he meant to ask something else as well. He ought to call Nicholas. Did Nicholas even know?

Jonathan bent down and kissed both his eyes, his cheeks, and his lips. Lorne's heart softened a little under the barrage. "You're going to tell them, every single day. We both are. Now," he gazed down quite sternly, "the ambulance will be here in about an hour. You haven't eaten anything since the birth, and if you don't eat, you won't be able to get all those IVs out. You're going to need two free arms."

"When will I be able to hold them?"

"We are going to have a meeting with a Doctor Gaven later this evening. He is going to explain everything to us, and we'll go from there."

"How come you don't know?" It seemed odd to Lorne.

"Because I'm an obstetrician not a pediatrician, and I was waiting until we both see them."

Lorne hissed in a surprised breath. "You haven't seen them?"

Jonathan shook his head. "Not since their birth. I wanted to, but I also wanted to meet them with you."

Lorne stared at Jonathan. "You did?" Something softened inside Lorne. *Maybe.*

He sat down on the bed and took Lorne's hand in his. "I know you think I've been forced into this. That a family isn't what I want, but it's actually the exact opposite. I used to have an omega as I was growing up."

"Declan."

Jonathan smiled. "Nana," he acknowledged resignedly. "The

thing is that's why I hate mating contracts. Because they have an expiration date."

"And you want permanency?" He wanted marriage. He'd even asked Lorne, and foolishly, Lorne had turned him down because he said he hadn't wanted that. Now he didn't know what he wanted.

"And we need to talk and arrange everything. I'm worried not pushing you into signing a contract made you think I didn't want one, and that couldn't be further from the truth, but we can and will do all of that later. First, we need to meet our babies." He brushed a finger down Lorne's cheek. The same way he had done since they met. "So *eat* something."

But Lorne couldn't help worrying. *Now* Jonathan wanted a contract. Was it because now he had the babies? He hadn't seemed in a hurry before. And the little warmth Lorne felt fizzled and died. Lorne managed some soup and a little bread, but after not eating for so long, it stuck in his throat. The nurse seemed pleased with him though, and he helped Lorne get changed and ready to move. It seemed very odd being able to stand even if the nurse did hover while he did so. He dutifully sipped a nutrition shake, and Jonathan came back in and unhooked his IVs. "We're leaving the line in until I see how the eating goes," he warned.

Trixie burst in still pinning on her ID badge. "I nearly missed you," she cried, and they hugged.

William also accompanied them to the ambulance, and Lorne groaned when he saw it even though he was in a wheelchair. Jonathan smiled. "You're still a patient."

Lorne sighed. "Will Nana be able to visit me?"

"She's already there," Jonathan laughed. "The second she found out you were transferring, she wanted to go make sure your room was comfortable."

Jonathan opened his mouth to say something else but stopped. Then he tried again. "I left a message with Nicholas's secretary this morning. He's in court all day. I've told Annabel, and she's very excited to see you. You'll probably be getting a visit from Bo and

Gabriel as soon as they are all okay. They all want to see you but understand they can't see the babies yet."

He wanted to ask questions, but they needed to be alone, and he was getting quite desperate to see his babies. It was weird. When he'd woken up, it was almost as if he'd been too scared to see them. He had tried to pretend it hadn't happened to keep from hearing any more bad news, now seeing them was all he could think about.

The ride didn't seem that long. Jonathan followed in his car, but Angela and Sam, the ambulance drivers, were really nice, and in no time, he was showing Angela the pictures he had of the babies. He also found out she was a trainee paramedic and very excited.

The ambulance stopped, and he wasn't even out before Jonathan appeared as solicitous to him as he was friendly to the ambulance drivers. Lorne watched him, trying to work out what he wanted, but then he forgot everything when he was wheeled into a ward. There were babies. At least five of them, and every one was being held or fed by their moms or omegas. Not that Lorne could tell the difference because they were all female. His breath hitched, and he turned away. It *hurt*.

"I'm sorry," Jonathan murmured. "This is the special post-natal annex. Every baby that's here has been in the neonatal ICU. They come here as the last step before going home. The good thing is everyone here knows what we are going through." Lorne nodded, comforted by the plural. Maybe it wasn't so bad. Jonathan wheeled him into a side room with a bed. He sniffed. It wasn't a big bed. And he knew he'd be essentially sleeping alone, and he turned his face into Jonathan as he bent down to help him out of the chair. Jonathan's arms came around him, and they hugged each other for a precious few seconds. He knew they had so much to sort out, decisions to make, but just for a moment, he wanted to pretend it was just them, and everything was going to be alright.

He looked up as a nurse came into the room. She stopped, a hand over her heart.

"Oh my goodness. Please tell me those adorable three are yours?

Of course, they are," she fussed. "With such good-looking daddies, how could they be anyone else's?" She beamed at Lorne as Jonathan settled him into bed. "My name is Aimee. We don't hold for last names here, even the doctors," she fake whispered and nodded at Jonathan who grinned good naturedly. "You settle in and get comfortable, and I'll let Andy—Doctor Gaven—know you're here." And she turned and left. Jonathan came and sat down next to him.

"How long will they let me stay here?"

"Your incision was healed by laser as is the norm, and the remnants of the pouch dissolve immediately when the blood flow is stopped to it. On paper, you are due to be discharged as soon as you're eating and drinking okay, but I know they have different rules here. Moms or dads go home, but often stay in overnight just before their babies go home, or longer if they have a special feeding or care regimen to get used to."

Which was exactly what Dr. Coulson said. "Do you know the doctor?"

"No, but he knows Gregory, and Gregory says he's good."

"That's a good recommendation," came a friendly voice from the door.

Jonathan grinned and stretched out a hand to the guy standing in khaki's and a shirt by the door. The only way you'd know he was a doctor was the stethoscope slung around his neck. "I'm Jonathan Owens, and this is my mate Lorne Austen."

Lorne shook the doctor's hand.

"Okay then," he started. "Hope is coming off the ventilator probably as early as tomorrow. She's going to continue gavage feeding—"

"Through a tube straight into her belly," Jonathan told Lorne, and Lorne nodded, feeling Jonathan's fingers clasp his own. He hung on tight.

Andy smiled. "Nicholas is actually doing well breathing wise even with his weight, and I expect him to be maybe a couple of days behind his sister." He paused and Lorne's heart sank.

"And Rowan?" Jonathan asked when Lorne couldn't seem to force words out.

"I'm sorry, but Rowan is a little more complicated."

He looked at Jonathan. "If you would like to see any of the notes or scans afterward, you are more than welcome, but essentially"—he focused back on Lorne—"everyone has two main heart arteries."

"Patent ductus arteriosus," Jonathan interrupted.

Andy nodded.

"Which is what?" Lorne demanded, looking at Jonathan in frustration.

"Sorry," he apologized and nodded to Andy as if he was to continue.

"The two main arteries usually separate before birth, but in some premature babies, this may need added help to happen."

Lorne blanched. "Surgery?"

"Unlikely." Andy shook his head. "Ninety percent of cases can be corrected with medication. We only proceed to surgery if it isn't successful."

"Can I see them?" Lorne nearly begged.

Andy nodded. "Of course. Aimee will take you both through and explain hand washing procedures. We have more babies than your three in there, so we have to be careful."

Lorne was frantic. Now he was so close, he couldn't wait, and he eagerly got in the chair Jonathan wheeled in. He wasn't even sure if he heard half of Aimee's instructions, but he knew Jonathan did, so he didn't worry. Jonathan pushed him through the swinging doors in the middle of the ward then through another set. He washed his hands. "Do I need gloves?"

Aimee shook her head. "No sweetie. Your babies need to feel you. But everyone else will wear gloves. Touch is very important. Especially on bare skin, and we'll show you how as we go along."

Lorne had tears in his eyes before he even got close enough to see them properly. "They're so small," he said weakly, terrified to touch them. Thin, wrinkly, but heartbreakingly beautiful and all theirs. He was shown how to put his hand through the hole in the side of the clear incubator and touch their hands and lay his hand gently over their heads. When Hope's then Nicholas's fingers curled around his own single finger, he wanted to bawl. He wanted to cry harder when Rowan's didn't. "Come on Rowley," Lorne murmured. "I'm here, and I know you're a fighter. You can't let Hope boss you around and steal all the cuddles."

"Rowley?" Jonathan murmured, and Lorne flushed but returned his smile. "And Nicky," he said determinedly.

Aimee was lovely with them both. She showed Lorne and Jonathan how to touch and where. She told them talking was important, and soon they hoped—maybe as early as tomorrow—at least Hope would be ready for her first cuddle.

Lorne would have stayed there forever and was upset when Jonathan eventually insisted he had to go back.

"You have to take care of yourself," Aimee cautioned. "You are going to be very busy once you get them home. Preemies have to be on a feeding schedule. None of them will be allowed to miss a feed or sleep through the night, even if they don't wake up." She squeezed Lorne's hands. "You can come in here at any time. But to be able to look after them, you need to be fit and well yourself."

"Nana will be here again tomorrow. She isn't allowed in the ICU and they have strict visiting times so she had to leave before we arrived, but she wants to see you and see if there's anything you need."

Lorne smiled, but the tears were there, just under the surface. So much to say and not enough. He didn't know where to start. He was utterly and completely overwhelmed.

Jonathan wheeled Lorne back to his room and helped him into bed. "How about if you try and get some rest then we can talk whenever you need to?"

Lorne nodded but curled up once he was in bed and closed his eyes. Jonathan woke him up a little later and practically force fed him. He roused himself enough to go see them one more time, but he could barely keep his eyes open once he got back in bed.

"You don't have to stay if you're busy," he said once he was lying down and because there was silence, he opened his eyes, thinking Jonathan had already left. The look on Jonathan's face made him open his eyes wider and immediately stretch his hand out. He cringed thinking how careless...how *hurtful* his words had been, and he immediately regretted them. "Jonathan?" Jonathan stared down at Lorne's hand as if it was almost a foreign object. "I need you."

"No, I don't think you do," he said bitterly, and he turned, saying he was going to the canteen. Lorne watched him go, desperately wanting to call him back but not being able to find the words he needed.

THIRTEEN

BREAKFAST WAS RUSHED. Lorne gobbled down his shake and some toast, ridiculously eager to see the babies. He knew they were all okay. Aimee had already reported in, but he was going to help with feeds and diapers, and he couldn't wait.

It was a little strained between him and Jonathan. Jonathan had been quiet—too quiet—and Lorne fretted that either it had been his careless, hurtful words last night, or that reality was sinking in, and Jonathan was wondering what the hell he'd gotten into.

He seemed to need to be everywhere at once when he got into the unit. They were still all on ventilators until the doctors made a decision later that morning, but Hope hung onto Jonathan's finger like it was a lifeline.

Funny, but Lorne knew exactly how she felt. The more he spent time with Jonathan, the more he *wanted* to spend time with him.

Jonathan had a visitor area he went to get showered and changed in later. He said he would quite like to take up Andy's offer and read the notes if Lorne wouldn't mind.

"Why should I mind?" Impetuously, he kissed him on the cheek. Jonathan looked delighted.

Not long after Jonathan had left, a middle-aged man appeared at his door. *He has a kind face* was Lorne's first impression. The man held out his hand and then hurriedly wiped the ink stain on his trousers before clasping Lorne's. "My name's Stephan Borowich, and I'm a clinical psychologist. Very pleased to meet you."

Lorne shook his hand, his brain going a million miles a minute. "What does a clinical psychologist do?" he asked suspiciously.

Stephan twinkled. "Straight jacket. Forced feeding. Padded cell."

Lorne laughed, but he was freaked out enough for it not to be funny.

"Can I be honest?"

Lorne's pulse sped up.

"You've been through hell."

Lorne started in surprise.

"I've been friends with Jonathan for a long time, but he doesn't know I'm here." He nudged him. "I've actually got the nurses keeping an eye out for him coming back."

"Why?" Lorne was confused as well as suspicious.

He sat down. "All preemie parents get a visit, but it was a colleague of mine who took a call from Jonathan yesterday that made him reach out to me."

Lorne inhaled sharply. What had Jonathan said? Didn't he think he could look after them? Did he think he was sick? "What—"

"Do you remember how you felt immediately after surgery?"

And that shut Lorne up. He remembered how completely disconnected he had felt. Like it had all happened to someone else.

"He cares about you," Stephan added. "This unit was full the day of surgery, or you might have been transferred even earlier. He told my colleague he was worried after all you'd been through with the birth, and the fact there were no babies with you was a huge let down."

Tears pricked Lorne's eyes. Jonathan had been right. He hadn't known how to describe what he was feeling except everything had been such a huge disappointment when he should have been doing cartwheels they were alive.

And that had made him ashamed.

How had Jonathan known?

"Which is completely and totally normal."

"It is?" Lorne raised his eyes and wiped his nose.

"Very much so. In fact, it was only because Jonathan is who he is that he recognized how you felt so quickly and moved heaven and earth to get you here."

And Lorne hadn't treated him very well. He'd dismissed him like he didn't care. Stephan passed him another tissue. "You're allowed to be angry. Resentful. Jealous every time a baby goes home. Frustrated because one of yours isn't doing the same. Blame yourself. Blame Jonathan. Blame the tooth fairy."

Lorne chuckled despite himself.

"No one's perfect. But the most important thing to learn is that you don't have to be. We understand," he added gently. "Everyone goes through degrees of the same." He smiled ironically. "My biggest challenge will be your alpha."

Lorne was confused. "But he's a doctor. He understands."

Stephan tried not to hyperventilate while he was laughing, and Lorne got the picture.

They chatted some more and somehow Stephan wheedled the whole story out of Lorne, and what worried him.

"I know this sounds a little silly, but it sounds like you need time to talk when you're not a patient and he's not your doctor. I'm guessing you haven't had any of that?"

Lorne shook his head. He remembered Jonathan scolding him gently and saying he had tried to find him. Had he wasted six months when they could have been getting to know each other better? "No, but I will today." He would.

Stephan stood up. "I can pop by any time just to see how things are going, and you can let Aimee know if you want to talk some more."

Lorne smiled gratefully. Stephan hadn't given him any answers, but he supposed it wasn't his job. He guessed the idea was he wanted to get Lorne to try and come up with his own. Except he didn't know where to start. Andy came into see them just as Jonathan arrived back from his shower and told them in another hour, when he had finished some discharge paperwork, they wanted to take Hope off the ventilator which thrilled Lorne, but Jonathan nodded sagely and gave him a quick pleased smile. Lorne decided to grab a quick shower while he was waiting, and Andy took out the IV ports so he could get in.

Then they were ready. Lorne felt so much better to be actually walking beside Jonathan rather than being pushed in a wheelchair. Andy said Hope would still have a small oxygen cannula under her nose for a few days, and Aimee patiently explained something called Kangaroo care which apparently had been around since years before the great wars.

Lorne sat down and undid his shirt as instructed. Aimee gently lifted Hope out and placed her on her belly on Lorne's chest, explaining that it was proven that all preemies receiving this sort of touch from their moms—or dads—thrived so much faster.

Lorne was entranced. Awed. And desperately and immediately in love. He lifted shining eyes to Jonathan who was sitting next to him, Hope clutching his finger. Lorne tried not to cry, but his heart was so full of love it kept spilling out. He spent an hour cuddling Hope, and then he sat next to Nicky while Jonathan sat next to Rowley. For the first time in forever, when they were all settled and Andy promised Nicky would be the next one off the ventilator in a few days, he felt a little hungry.

They walked back to Lorne's room together, holding hands as if they had been together for years, and Jonathan pushed the door opened and paused in stunned surprise. Lorne gaped because he had honestly never seen so many flowers in his entire life. Jonathan walked up to the first basket arrangement and read the card. Then he simply turned on his heel and left the room. Lorne picked it up.

Many Congratulations – Nicholas,
Suzanna, and Sophie

It didn't say anything too bad, and Lorne bristled slightly. They were his family, had been his family for a lot of years, Jonathan couldn't expect him to simply pretend they didn't exist. He went to the next one and smiled at the baby elephant with the flowers held in its trunk and saw Suzanna had written that one. He read the card from Sophie and smiled at the drawing she had included of herself. She was very talented. Then he spotted the small parcel and picked it up. He recognized the sender's address as Nicholas's office and managed to get it open.

It was a cell phone.

And there was a note in it from Nicholas saying all the numbers he knew were preprogrammed in, including his, and he urged him to call him as soon as he could.

Lorne remembered the young boy who had grown into a young man who Lorne loved very much and pressed the button to dial the number.

"Lorne?" Nicholas sounded worried. "How are you? How are the babies?"

He smiled and filled him in. Nicholas was planning on traveling up that weekend, and Lorne promised to tell him where he was staying so they could meet.

"Carmichael's coming up?"

Lorne jumped at Jonathan's terse words and turned around. He gazed at him and nodded.

Jonathan glanced at the phone in Lorne's hand. "I'm sorry I should have got you one of those."

Suddenly, Lorne couldn't stand it any longer. He'd been expecting Jonathan to be angry, but he wasn't. He just sounded sad. Lorne was being incredibly unfair to someone who had cared for him and been prepared to open his heart for their new family.

"I'm sorry. They were all the family I had for a very long time. I—"

But Jonathan closed the gap between them. "No, *I'm* sorry. I'm a stupid, jealous fool that is old enough to know better."

Lorne's heart swelled. "J-jealous?"

"Uh-huh." Jonathan pulled him closer, and Lorne rested his head on Jonathan's shoulder. "I told you three weeks ago you belonged to me. Was I wrong?"

Lorne lifted his head. He wanted to belong to Jonathan. He wanted it so much. "And what about the day when none of you need me anymore?"

"Never gonna happen," Jonathan said. "And I can put that in as many contracts as you want. Nicholas is a lawyer. I'm sure he can come up with whatever makes you happy."

"Mating contracts only last fifteen years."

Jonathan huffed. "I don't know what you want me to say. I've offered everything I can think of." He rubbed gentle circles up and down Lorne's back. "Why don't we get something to eat, go check on our little terrors, and then go home? They will discharge you today."

Lorne nodded. He quite liked the sound of all that.

They grabbed some lunch, and Lorne ate nearly all of it much to Jonathan's obvious delight. Then they went back to the unit and managed cuddle time with Hope and quiet time with Nicky and Rowley.

"You do know, he'll hate that name when he's older, don't you?" Jonathan was watching Lorne hold Hope on his bare chest, and he had his own hand cupped on top of Rowley's head like Aimee had shown them. As much as preemies needed touch, some very little ones could find too much overwhelming, so they were being cautious.

"They're doing incredibly well."

Lorne looked up to see Andy. "We're going to start gavage feeding with Nicholas tomorrow. Take him off the ventilator." He looked at Lorne. "His oxygen tubing may look a little different to Hope's but don't be alarmed. They are just at different stages."

Jonathan nodded toward one of the other incubators that held a baby. "I haven't noticed that little one have any visitors."

Andy followed his gaze. "Because she was found abandoned in the waiting room. We can't get anything from CCTV, and no one has come forward. She's five weeks early and will soon be ready to be adopted. I'm sure they have Alphas already lined up."

Just then, the door opened, and Lorne recognized the orderly he had met at the clinic. He'd worked the nights with Maggie. "Cal?"

The young man looked up at his name and smiled, walking over to them quickly. "Oh my goodness." He gazed at the babies. "Maggie will be so jealous when I tell her I've seen them."

"I didn't know you worked here as well?" Jonathan said.

Cal flushed, seemingly painfully shy. "I don't, Alpha," he said respectfully. "I'm a volunteer mom."

"A volunteer *mom?*" Lorne repeated.

Cal nodded and gestured to the baby they had just been talking about. "I get to be a mom or *dad* I guess, with her until she gets her very own." But the way Cal said it so enviously, Lorne knew he wished he was more than a volunteer.

"Congratulations to you both," Cal added, and Lorne watched as he washed his hands and put on a gown like the nursing staff. He soon had the little darling in his arms, and Aimee handed him a bottle for her to suck.

"That's amazing," Jonathan remarked. "What a good thing to do."

But it would be so hard, thought Lorne, and he wondered how many babies Cal had given up? He was handling that one like he had plenty of practise.

They stayed quite a few hours until Lorne was trying unsuccess-fully to hide his yawns, and Jonathan led him un-protesting back to his room. "They are happy to discharge you."

Lorne glanced up at Jonathan. "And I'm guessing they need the bed."

Jonathan nodded. "They do, but it's getting late. I'm sure I can swing another night." But Lorne remembered how empty he had felt without his babies. He didn't want someone else in that position. "No," he reached out for Jonathan's hand. "Let's go home."

And Jonathan's face lit up at Lorne's words.

JONATHAN WAS THRILLED. At least he thought he was. The last few days—hell the last three weeks—had been such an emotional roller coaster he didn't know which end was up. And he wasn't used to that. His life had been about control and planning since he was fifteen. To be honest, he'd been a little bit like that as a child, but it hadn't seemed unusual in his house.

Turning down the job which was on paper what he had worked for all his life hadn't been as hard of a decision as he thought, and he felt a little guilty he was letting down the omegas who would benefit, but he couldn't in all conscience be a part of something he thought was morally wrong on such a basic level.

And he had friends. There was no reason why they couldn't look at doing something on a smaller scale to help omegas here. He knew a lot of doctors who would give their services for free. Maybe they could start something? Maybe Lorne would like to get Nicholas involved? He could cope with that.

Jonathan carried everything to the car. Because of the flowers, he had to make a couple of trips, but when he came back in, it was to see Lorne hugging Aimee.

She was tutting at his obviously damp eyes. "You can see them anytime. Even when Jonathan has to go back to work, he can drop you here first."

"He will have his own car." Jonathan joined them. It had been one of the calls he had made over a week ago. There was no way he could get three child seats plus everything else in his BMW coupe. Gabe was pleased with Bo's minivan, so he had ordered the same model. His eyebrow rose at the strange look he was getting from Lorne. "What?"

"You're going to let me drive?" Lorne said in utter awe.

"Of course," Jonathan said, failing to see what the fuss was about. Then he twigged. "You can't drive?" And he could have kicked himself when Lorne flushed and shook his head. He hadn't meant it as a criticism. "Hey," he tipped Lorne's chin up with his finger. "I guarantee you will be a better driver than I am. I'm sure you have a ton more patience. We'll have you driving everywhere in no time." And because he could, he kissed Lorne's startled lips.

And for the first time in a few days, he had other thoughts.

Lorne was quiet as they drove away from the hospital, but Jonathan knew he would be tired. He'd managed to call his nan from the car while he was packing it with flowers, and she would have some food ready for them. "I need to warn you," he suddenly blurted out.

Lorne glanced at him in bemusement. "Warn me about what?"

"The state of the house. I have a cleaning company, but it needs so many repairs amongst all the other things that are breaking down. I was always just going to sell, but..."

Lorne gazed at him as they turned off the highway. "But you have Nana to consider."

"Not just," Jonathan said firmly, and Lorne smiled.

But when he pulled up, Jonathan honestly wondered what had possessed him to bring Lorne here. It looked worse seeing it through someone else's eyes, but before he could offer another apology, or any sort of excuse, Nana appeared on the steps and held her arms out as Lorne nearly ran into them. He pulled out Lorne's few bags and followed him into the kitchen.

Then stopped, wondering if he had driven to the wrong house. The place was warm, clean, and smelled divine.

Lorne inhaled appreciatively. "What is that?"

"My homemade soup," Nana shared with a pleased smile and an arched brow at Jonathan. "Jonathan wanted you to feel welcome, so he's had a cleaning company going through the whole house after the roof was repaired last week. It's badly in need of decorating and a lot of refurbishing, but that's something you'll need to think on."

Lorne turned to Jonathan with such an eager smile Jonathan could have quite happily danced around the kitchen.

But he was selling the house.

Or was he?

Maybe that wasn't such a good idea. The memories he had steadfastly turned his back on could easily be replaced with better ones. After all it was huge. A large fenced yard. He would have to check out the schools—

Nana fussed over Lorne while Jonathan ran up to his room and stowed Lorne's case. He looked around at the small space. It had been his room since he was fourteen, but the master three doors down was huge. There were also two rooms opposite that would make a lovely nursery. Excited, he nearly ran back downstairs.

Lorne was sitting at the large oak table, but he looked in danger of falling asleep. Jonathan sat quietly while Nana fussed, but as soon as Lorne didn't look like he was going to eat anymore, he spoke up. "Lorne. Come on. Bed." He kissed his nan and said he would cook breakfast, but Lorne needed his sleep, and steered him upstairs. "The room's basic, but we can sort that out later," he said, pushing Lorne inside and turning him around gently.

"Would you like a bath?"

The heat that flared in Lorne's eyes was apparent, even to him, and he felt almost as if they had come full circle. He soon had the tub filling and came back in to find Lorne struggling to pull off his socks. "Careful," he admonished. "Laser healing is fabulous. Back in the old days they even had to sew wounds up with a needle and thread." Lorne stopped with a gasp.

"You're kidding?"

Jonathan shook his head. "Nope. I could tell you stories that would make your hair curl, but what I'm trying to say is sometimes not having a visible wound makes you forget you had one very recently. You're swollen. Still tender, and bending down to do socks"—Jonathan kneeled down in front of Lorne—"is my job for a few days."

Lorne flushed while Jonathan very carefully took his socks off, brushing his knuckle under the arches and making Lorne's eyes flutter shut. His lips formed a little moue, but he made no sound. Jonathan eased both of Lorne's arms out of his sweater and T-shirt and gazed at the light sprinkling of hair over his chest. "I was almost jealous of Hope today," he whispered, which made Lorne's eyes fly open, and Jonathan leaned forward to brush Lorne's lips with his own. The sigh that came from Lorne as they touched was very good. As if he was giving himself over to Jonathan.

He eased him upright then unbuckled his pants. "Did you read the pamphlet you were given?"

Lorne dipped his head, but Jonathan could see the redness bloom on his neck. "No penetration for up to four weeks until my passage loosens." Jonathan grinned. It had been a little more blunt than that, but however Lorne needed to explain, he was good with.

"Uh-huh," Jonathan murmured and kissed his shoulders. "Which gives me a lot of time to prep you."

Lorne raised his head in astonishment, and Jonathan grinned helplessly. It was a lovely idea. "And coincidentally, I have at least a week before I need to go back to the clinic." He trailed a finger along Lorne's jaw, and Lorne leaned in to the touch. Jonathan took his hand and led him into the bathroom and stripped quickly, stepping in and holding his hand out for Lorne. Lorne smiled. "It should be me bathing you this time."

"And while that's a lovely idea, and one I'm definitely going to take you up on in the future, you are nearly dead on your feet."

Lorne sighed because it was true; though he didn't want to disappoint Jonathan, so he got in, groaning in sheer relief as his body sank into the warm water, and he relaxed back on Jonathan. His eyes slid shut nearly immediately. "I don't know how I'm tired all the time. I've been in bed for three weeks, and it's not like I'm actually looking after three babies yet." He bit his lip, and Jonathan kissed his neck.

"Okay, so up to forty-eight hours ago, your body had been working overtime to feed three babies in a system only designed for one. You have had surgery twice, once as an emergency. You had to be transferred to another hospital then you were discharged. That's on top of the worry for our three babies."

Lorne chuckled tiredly. "Well, I guess when you put it like that."

Jonathan kissed him again and picked up the sponge and some soap. He seemed to remember a certain someone had some very sensitive nipples, and he deliberately let his hand stray. The shiver he got as a result was very gratifying. "Shh," he soothed as Lorne's hand moved as if he felt he needed to do something, and Lorne relaxed again. Jonathan washed him everywhere he could reach. He wasn't sure whether to be pleased or offended when Lorne's head lolled to one side, showing he was asleep. He let a little bit more hot water in the bath and relaxed back imagining a lifetime of coming home to evenings like this.

After a while, when the water was cooling once more, he woke Lorne up who began stammering apologies which he shushed again simply by kissing him. He had Lorne dry and tucked up in bed in no time, finally curling around his omega and closing his own eyes.

FOURTEEN

JONATHAN MUST HAVE BEEN STILL asleep. In no reality he knew of did he ever wake up to the glorious sensation of someone sucking his dick. He groaned appreciatively and widened his legs as Lorne's hand explored gently, cupping his balls and tracing a finger on his taint. He was hard and aching and simultaneously torn by needing to get off and wanting to draw things out.

No, he wanted a kiss and slid his hands under Lorne's arms, but at that second, Lorne seemed to swallow him down. He groaned louder. "You are so good at this." In seconds—or was it hours because time seemed to hold little relevance—his balls had drawn up, and he was panting his release into that too talented mouth.

"That was phenomenal," he murmured then helped Lorne ease his way up and plastered a scorching kiss onto Lorne's swollen lips. Lorne murmured in the back of his throat. A sound that went straight to Jonathan's cock, and it jerked appreciatively. Jonathan chuckled. "You wake me up like that more often, and I'll soon forget I'm thirty-five next month."

Lorne tutted, called him old man, and then rolled out of the way when Jonathan went to tickle him in punishment. "Why don't you get a shower and rearrange your things?" Jonathan suggested. Lorne hadn't even unpacked last night. "Put anything anywhere, and I'll go rustle up some breakfast. Come down when you're ready." Lorne brushed a sweet kiss on Jonathan's lips, and his dick made another valiant effort to respond. "Or we can just go back to bed?"

Lorne chuckled. "We have baby cuddling duty in just over an hour."

"At least I get to look at your bare chest." He waggled his eyebrows, and Lorne grinned.

He wanted to start every morning like that. Well, not necessarily the dick sucking, although that had been amazing, but the closeness, the teasing. The welcoming of someone into your space and enjoying having them there. He'd forgotten what that felt like. Or had he ever known?

Nana was just boiling the kettle for tea when he came into the kitchen, and she reached up so he could drop a kiss on her cheek. She eyed him carefully. "Being mated suits you." Jonathan grinned and went to put the coffee on. He leaned on the counter and looked out at the back yard, imagining the size of the swing set he could get in there. A tree house would be amazing, and it wasn't like he didn't have room.

He glanced back and looked at Nana. "I'm thinking of not selling."

She smiled. "Really?"

"I'm going to talk to Lorne when he has a second to breathe."

She brewed her tea. "I was looking at some of the cottages in the village with Annabel a week ago."

"You were?" Jonathan was stunned. "But—"

Nana smiled. "I'm thrilled you're thinking of staying here, but you don't need me cluttering up the place. I can visit. You can visit." But Jonathan was already shaking his head as he walked towards her.

"Absolutely not. You held me together when I was falling apart. You're as big a part of this family as everyone else, and we want you here."

She reached up and cupped his cheek. "I'm not going to move out next week or anything. Let's see what Lorne thinks."

But Jonathan knew what Lorne would think. Family was important to him. There was no way he would want Nana living anywhere else. "Of course," Jonathan added slyly. "I understand if you think it's going to be too crazy around here. I mean three babies are a lot of work at your—*umphh*." He grinned. The punch on his arm had been more than he needed, but the reaction of an indignant seventy-five-year-old had been exactly what he was hoping for.

"What happened to breakfast?" Lorne teased from the doorway.

Nana huffed and stepped back from Jonathan's embrace. "He only does pancakes anyway. In over thirty years, that's all I've ever seen him cook."

Jonathan was outraged. "But they're good pancakes." Laughing, they all ate breakfast together.

TWO DAYS LATER, Lorne was secretly thrilled at how things were going. He had slept every night in Johnathon's arms and spent all day with the babies. *I could get used to it.* And he could—so easily. For the first time, he let himself hope that this was what his life would be like. They walked hand in hand into the unit, and Lorne was delighted to see Professor Denholm talking to Andy.

He was less delighted to see Dr. Coulson looking at the charts, but he knew she didn't work here and would be leaving soon. He shook hands but didn't bother to acknowledge Dr. Coulson as she didn't look up until Jonathan greeted her

He glanced over to the incubators as normal and hurried to greet his babies. "Nicholas is now off the ventilator," Aimee announced.

Lorne could see, and he looked back at Jonathan, but he was talking to Andy.

"And we want you to feed Hope. It takes a tremendous amount of effort to suck so we will continue the gavage feeding in between."

"Congratulations, Lorne," Professor Denholm followed him as he placed a careful hand over Rowley.

Lorne glanced back. "I never got the chance to say thank you."

The professor beamed. "You are entirely welcome, and just between me and you, the medical community are going to love reading the report I'm currently doing. No names obviously," he added. He glanced over to where Andy, Jonathan, and Dr. Coulson were standing talking. "Of course, I will credit your mate. Both of them will be able to pick and choose any job now." He patted Lorne's back, admired Rowley, and then wandered back to the other doctors.

Lorne watched him go, wondering why he suddenly had a bad feeling but then dismissed it as his hormones still being out of whack. He greeted Nicky and, after a few minutes, lifted Hope out and settled her on his chest. She snuggled in seeming content.

"Do you mind if I leave you for a few minutes?" Jonathan asked, walking up to them and bending down to kiss Hope on her head. "I was just asked to consult on a patient."

Lorne shook his head, knowing being a doctor was as essential to Jonathan as oxygen, and lifted his face to receive a kiss which Jonathan immediately gave him. Jonathan brushed Lorne's jaw with his finger. "I won't be long."

He watched them go and barely a second later he saw Cal come in the door. Cal smiled immediately when he saw Lorne then he glanced toward the baby he had been caring for the last few days and his face fell.

Damn, Lorne thought. She wasn't there, and he had been so absorbed in his own little darlings he'd never noticed.

"I'm sorry, Cal," Aimee bustled over. "I tried to call you this morning. She was transferred last night to meet her prospective new family. She doesn't need NICU now, so it made more sense. Lovely family." Aimee added and went to answer the phone on the desk. She didn't see the disappointment on Cal's face. The hurt. The *weariness* almost.

"Cal?" Lorne called out. "I don't suppose you could help me?"

Cal glanced over in confusion almost as if Lorne was speaking another language.

"Unless you're busy," Lorne faltered. He was too impulsive sometimes.

Cal shook himself and walked over. "Of course. What do you need?"

"Actually," Lorne nodded over to where Nicky was wriggling, knowing he was working himself up. "Would you mind awfully holding Hope so I can grab him?"

And Cal's face lit up. "I'd love to."

Lorne mentally patted himself on the back. Cal was approved to touch the babies and seeing as how his little one had gone, Lorne didn't have to worry about cross infection. He settled Hope into Cal's arms and went to fetch Nicky who quieted again almost immediately.

"It suits you," he nodded to where Cal was murmuring softly to Hope. Cal bit his lip, and Lorne desperately wanted to ask if he was an omega but didn't feel he could. He could be a beta, but Lorne doubted it. "It must be hard coming here, caring, and then seeing them go."

Cal glanced up. "I'm happy for them though. She will have a lovely family."

Lorne nodded, and they were silent for a while.

"You're incredibly lucky," Cal said after a few minutes which gave Lorne the opening he needed.

"It will be your turn soon enough," he chuckled. "I'm probably at least ten years older than you." *Maybe more.*

Cal shook his head. "I can't have children. I was in an accident a long time ago, and they had to remove the pouch along with half my stomach." He shrugged. "I grew up knowing I'll never be able to get pregnant. It's no big deal."

But it was. Lorne could see it was. "Well, I'm going to need lots of help," he said. "How often do you get to be here?"

"I work four nights a week at the clinic. I call in here after the nights and on my day off."

"Do you sleep?" Lorne teased, and Cal grinned.

"Sleep is overrated." He smirked. "But I guess you'll find that out soon enough."

Cal stayed with Hope until she was asleep then reluctantly left to get some sleep himself. Lorne settled Nicky back in his incubator then spent some time talking and holding Rowley's hand. He was still on a ventilator, but they were thinking they might take him off in another week.

He looked up as the door opened, shocked to see Dr. Coulson back and on her own. He didn't really understand what, as an arterial specialist, she was doing here. There were two other babies here, but he hadn't met their moms or omegas yet, and he knew he wasn't allowed to touch them.

But, ignoring him as usual, she wandered over to Hope's charts and picked them up.

The sudden terrifying thought that there might be something else wrong with Hope that he didn't know about hit him like a brick wall. "Is everything all right?"

She nodded, and Aimee came over. "Lorne? Message from Jonathan. He's gone to pick up his nan now those three are allowed direct family visitors." Lorne smiled his thanks. Nana would be thrilled, and she may be back in time to help with Hope's next feed.

He took a breath and focused back on Rowley. The small cough from Dr. Coulson to get his attention surprised him. She gave a tight smile when he looked at her. "You must be pleased with how they are all doing."

"Yes, I'm very grateful to everyone for their care." And he was. Much as he didn't care for the woman, they might not be alive if she wasn't good at her job. There was an awkward pause because she was still standing there, and Lorne didn't know if he was expected to talk or not.

"I'm sorry if I've been a bit brusque since you were admitted." She forced a small, self-deprecating laugh. "I'm afraid my bedside manner needs a little work."

It needed a complete overhaul in Lorne's opinion, but he wasn't going to snub what seemed to be an attempt at civility. "I'm fortunate you have taken an interest in my babies."

She nodded as if she was agreeing with him, and he hid a smile. "I admit of course to a certain selfishness, I suppose."

Because she wanted Professor Denholm's recommendation, he guessed. It made sense she would want to shine. "Will a new job mean you have to relocate?"

She frowned and dropped the chart. She picked it up and put it on the table her expression irritated, and Lorne wondered what he'd said that was wrong.

"Of course, we would have to relocate," she said impatiently.

We? Who was *we?* Still trying to be tactful Lorne plastered on a polite smile. "I imagine your family are thrilled at the opportunity."

She tilted her head and gazed at him with a puzzled air. "Hasn't Jonathan said anything to you?"

Lorne felt his pulse pick up. "Said anything?"

She sighed. A huge put-upon noise as if she couldn't trust anyone else to do a simple task. "The new post is a team position for us both. Jonathan would be the first to admit his talents are completely wasted here, and I don't object to his grandmother having some sort of apartment off our main house." She mused to herself. "We would make it large enough to accommodate you of course, and the children until they grew old enough to be in civilized company."

She pursed her lips as if considering something else. "Jonathan admitted to me he regretted his impulsive decision to end our engagement." Lorne froze. It was as if every drop of blood in his veins was congealing. His heart thumped to try and force his sluggish body to co-operate. Dr. Coulson? Jonathan had been engaged to *her?*

"I understand, of course. The news his grandmother had deteriorated and he needed to leave his job and move here was a shock to everyone." She shook her head in exasperation. "I can forgive him his impulsiveness, I suppose." She brightened. "And we can always negotiate another contract after your initial term on the off-chance

Jonathan's grandmother is still alive and needs someone to care for her. You would be well compensated."

Lorne looked up in a complete daze.

"Of course, he didn't say anything earlier because it may have proved unnecessary."

"You mean if he doesn't take the job?" Lorne guessed.

"No, I mean—" She looked at Rowley, and Lorne died a little bit more.

"You mean if the babies didn't survive," he whispered in defeat.

She lifted her hand as if she was going to pat his awkwardly. Lorne moved his own out of the way.

"Well. You won't be tied down, and I suppose as you are an older omega you would be heading for retirement when the children reach fifteen." As if that was supposed to make it better. And understanding made Lorne's eyes smart. That was why Jonathan hadn't ever mentioned the mating contract again. His breath hitched, and he closed his eyes as they stung. He'd thought Jonathan was different, but he should have known better. He opened his eyes helpless to stop the tears forming and hoping she would blame his emotions on hormones.

She looked at him suddenly focused. "I'm surprised not to see your attorney. He seemed a very capable man when we met." With that, she walked away.

Lorne glanced around at the quiet ward, suddenly and completely bereft of something he'd never had in the first place. The nurses were huddled around the desk, handing on information to the next team on duty. All the babies were sleeping.

No one could see the huge bloodstain on the floor where his heart had ripped open. The tattered remnants of his dignity peeled away, shredded, and laid bare along with any self-respect he ever had. He'd even convinced himself Jonathan had been giving him time to sign the contract when all he had been doing was hedging his bets.

Lorne gazed down at Rowley. He'd been so devastated he'd missed the tiny automatic curling of little fingers around his own.

The movement he had been longing for for three days had come and gone, and Lorne had been so mired in misery he hadn't felt it.

And that made him angry, more than anything else. He pushed his other hand into his pocket and his fingers closed around the phone Nicholas had given him, and he pressed the button for the first saved number. Nicholas answered immediately.

"Lorne? I've just pulled of the Northern Expressway. I was just going to drop off my bag at the hotel then call and see if you were at the hospital."

There was a pause while Lorne tried to speak.

"Lorne?" Nicholas's voice changed. "What is it?"

"I'm at the hospital. Please come and get me." His throat closed on the last word, and he heard Nicholas swear.

"I'm on my way."

He was on his way. Lorne stood, bent and kissed the tiny fingers that were holding one of his, and apologized for having to let go. "But not for long, Rowley," he promised and went around to each baby and made the same vow. He would get them from Jonathan. Sign anything Nicholas needed to make it happen. No one was ever going to take his family from him again.

FIFTEEN

JONATHAN PULLED up at home just as Nana opened the front door. He grinned. He sometimes thought she had a tracking chip installed in him as a child. He couldn't wait to see her arms full of the babies. He was confident that between them all, she wouldn't be moving out. She smiled eagerly and handed over a bag with three huge gifts in them and her knitting. She had been working on matching hats for them to wear while they were in the incubators.

"All ready? Did the other gift arrive?"

"In the bag," Nana confirmed.

It had taken some arranging. It had also taken some work trying to find Lorne's ring size, and they'd had to take an educated guess in the end. Nana was going to be on baby duty while Jonathan whisked Lorne into the canteen.

Okay, so that wasn't the most romantic place for a proposal, but he knew Lorne wouldn't want to leave the babies, and Aimee had introduced him to the canteen manager who was thrilled with the idea and had managed to set them up a special table in the corner behind a partition. He had fibbed and told Lorne he'd been asked to do a consult on a patient when, really, he had been racing around like an insane man trying to get his ridiculous, impetuous idea formed into something resembling organization. And they had all been on it.

Well. *All* except Anne. If his day had one cloud, it had been telling Anne he wasn't taking the job and having to deal with her disappointment. Apparently, there was more than her in the running for the position, and the other specialist had his own team so she wouldn't get a look in. He soon got the message it had been a joint offer or nothing.

Which made him feel awful, but Gregory had assured him he would put out feelers and get her another offer soon enough. It wasn't his fault she had already given notice at her other position, so confident was she that Jonathan would say yes.

And talking to Andy afterward, he found out there were a few other doctors that were willing to give their help for free, so his idea of a male omega birthing clinic was starting to take root.

The biggest challenge had been to come up with something to show Lorne he was serious, and it had taken every bit of ingenuity he had. And Gabe, or rather Emma his attorney sister, had spent forty-eight hours making sure the idea was legal, but apparently, all it needed was his signature.

So rare it was unheard of, but it might just be the exact thing he needed to make Lorne trust him. He wasn't stupid. He knew—hoped —Lorne was half way in love with him.

He tried to concentrate on driving. Having a wreck was the last thing he needed.

"Don't worry," Nana laid a hand on his arm. "The boy loves you. He just needs to trust you, and if what is in those boxes mean as much to him as I think they will, we will have a wedding to plan."

Jonathan didn't care. I mean, he did obviously, but Lorne could have any wedding he wanted. Hell, he'd hire out a cathedral and turn up in a tux if that was what it took. So long as he had his family at the end of the day, none of the rest mattered. Whatever Lorne wanted, he would have.

Jonathan pulled into the parking lot next to the neonatal unit and turned off the engine. He climbed out and went around to the other door to help his nan. "Jonathan," she urged in an odd voice which made him look up.

And his eyes clashed with a pair of angry violet blue ones. "Lorne?" He took in Nicholas and his sisters Suzanna and Sophie. He'd forgotten they were coming this weekend but no matter. They could join in the celebration afterwards. He pasted on a smile and stalked forward only to falter when Lorne made an odd sound and stepped behind Nicholas.

As if he was getting out of the way.

As if he needed Nicholas's protection.

As if he needed Nicholas's protection from *him*.

He shook his head because that made no sense, and from the corner of his eye, he saw Nana drawing the girls away and asking them to carry the presents.

"Lorne, sweetheart?" He stopped again in confusion. Why was he leaving? Maybe Aimee didn't give him the message. "Sorry, I'm late back. I was hoping to see you on your own for just a little while then you can visit with the family."

Lorne stared at him and deliberately took a step so he was facing Jonathan with no barrier. "How could you?" The words were whispered but every bit as forceful as if he had shouted them.

Jonathan frowned. "I don't understand."

"I know. She told me."

"She?" Jonathan repeated in bewilderment and took a step towards Lorne only to be blocked by Nicholas. "What the hell?"

"Keep away from my mate," he clipped out.

Jonathan laughed. He hadn't meant it was funny, more ridiculous. "Look, I have no idea what joke—"

"It isn't funny," Lorne interrupted.

"No," Jonathan nodded becoming irritated. "It isn't especially as you're *my*—" And then he knew. Comprehension and utter horror flashed through him. "You're going with Nicholas." After all they had gone through, Lorne still didn't trust him. He had chosen Nicholas.

Jonathan stumbled and leaned heavily against the car. He didn't know how his legs were holding him up.

"Lorne will be filing for desertion, and the right to keep the babies. He will be mated to me as early as tomorrow, and the proper contract will be filed with the omega administration services. Lorne has insisted you are able—should you wish—to keep visiting the children both while they are here and when we move. I, however, would prefer you put that request in writing via your attorney so a proper visiting schedule can be drawn up, especially while they are still in the NICU. I'm sure you can appreciate Lorne doesn't want to be here when you are."

Jonathan didn't reply. He wasn't sure he could remember how to form words. He was barely aware of Anne hurrying to the car and kindly offering to take them both home as his nan didn't drive any longer. He supposed it was lucky she was there. Not that he cared about that either.

Tears rolled down Lorne's face while Sophie clutched his hand and murmured soothing noises. He had been so angry. So furious until the second they had left the hospital and they had seen Jonathan. Then all he had felt was hurt. A deep betrayal he had always promised himself never to feel again. He wasn't sure how he had managed to stand firm and not rush to Jonathan and beg him.

But beg him for what? There was nothing Jonathan could offer that he wanted.

A home?

Nicholas would provide that.

Security?

Ditto.

A family? He bit his lip and twisted his hands together. He had one. It might not be what he had started believing he might get in the last few days, but he would love and protect them with his life. He knew Nicholas would be good to him. He intended to tell him tonight exactly what he wanted and what he didn't want from a contract. All he wanted was Nicholas's name and friendship. He was free to marry. Free to take any lover he wanted. He was a young man, and Lorne certainly wouldn't stop him. And he supposed, if Nicholas met someone and they had children, he would have more children to care for.

He was so sorry about Nana though. He had started to love her as much as her son.

Love. And his heart broke all over again.

"Don't cry," Sophie said softly, and he smiled at her and eventually dried his eyes. No more crying now. He was done, especially when Nicholas pulled into a drive-through, much to the twins delight. Lorne managed to force some food down his throat even though he wasn't hungry. They were all being very sweet, and after the twins were settled, he took a cab back to the hospital, insisting Nicholas stay with his sisters.

Lorne returned for the afternoon. Aimee wasn't working, and he was relieved. He wasn't sure if anyone knew what had happened outside, and he was immensely relieved that Jonathan or Nana weren't there. Hope was guzzling her milk like it was her last meal and that more than anything gave him a little optimism for his future. Another day and Nicky would start bottle feeding. Six more days and they hoped Rowley might be able to breathe on his own. He absolutely couldn't wait for his first cuddle with his son.

Nicholas and the girls collected him from the hospital around five, and they all went for something to eat. Sophie was ridiculously excited to meet her new brothers and sister as she insisted they were even though Suzanna said technically they were her nephews and nieces.

Or maybe not. Not even Lorne could work out that relationship. And when they got back to the hotel, the girls were desperate for Lorne to unwrap the presents they had brought with them.

Lorne smiled at the cute romper suits for preemies, the rattles, and more teddies. He opened a box Suzanna passed over and lifted the lid. Confused he pulled out a piece of paper and a hand knitted hat. A tiny one just the size for one of the babies. He looked at Suzanna. "Is this from you?" The hat was handmade, and he didn't think they knew how.

She shook her head. "No, they were what the old lady at the hospital gave us."

Lorne froze. Nicholas winced in understanding. "I'm sorry. I thought they were one of theirs." He gestured to the pile of gifts. "I'll take it." He reached out, but Lorne had opened the piece of paper.

"What's this?" he asked, not understanding what he was looking at.

Nicholas gently took the piece of paper from him and scanned it. "Suze, is there more than just this one?" And of course there was. The nice old lady had given them three, all with small handmade hats and all with identical pieces of paper.

"What does it mean?" Lorne asked.

Nicholas read the other two. "I would have to check, but they've been notarized. They seem genuine."

"What are they?" He didn't understand what he was looking at.

Nicholas put them together and handed them over. "They are adoption certificates for Hope, Nicholas, and Rowan."

"But Jonathan doesn't need to adopt them. They're his already."

Nicholas's smile twisted. "I'm not even sure if you are aware of what you just said, but these certificates give up Jonathan's legal right to the babies and name you as legal guardian."

Lorne shook his head. "Can he do that?"

And Nicholas smiled. "Yes. It's an amazing gesture, but by doing this, he is saying that the babies are yours. You still have to mate an alpha in the eyes of the law to keep them, but we won't have to take him to court. You can mate any alpha you want to."

"But why? I mean..." But Lorne didn't know what he meant.

"I think," Nicholas drew out the words as if formulating them at the same time. "I think you might be wrong. This doesn't seem to me the actions of someone who wants to force you into anything." He gazed at Lorne and then leaned back in his chair. "I just hope that it turns out that Jonathan's biggest crime is not getting his finger out of his ass and actually talking to you. We didn't get much chance to talk ourselves with the girls being there, but do you trust the source of this information? Who told you Jonathan was getting married?"

Lorne gulped. And everything coalesced in his mind. How Dr. Coulson never spoke to him except to criticize. How suddenly she wanted to be friendly. How she was the most ambitious person he had ever met.

And how Jonathan had done nothing but open his arms, his home, and his heart for them.

"What have I done?" he whispered in complete and utter horror, knowing he had possibly just made the biggest mistake of his life.

SIXTEEN

LORNE COULDN'T STAY at the hotel if his life had depended on it. Nicholas offered to ask Annabel to watch the girls and accompany him, but Lorne knew this was one conversation he had to have on his own. No hiding behind anyone. He needed to go to Jonathan's house but got a cab to the hospital first.

Maybe seeing his babies would give him the courage he needed. He had asked Nicholas to print him out a simple mating contract off the internet. One that gave him no legal recourse whatsoever. Lorne was shaking. Everything could go so wrong, it wasn't even funny, but he had to show Jonathan he trusted him, and there was only one thing he could think of.

He smiled at Peter and Joanna, the two nurses on duty in the unit. Saddened that Aimee wasn't there because he would have appreciated her air of confidence and walked towards the incubators.

And stopped.

Because the babies weren't on their own. Jonathan was sitting with his eyes closed, and Nicky was sprawled asleep on his chest. He cracked open his eyelids, hearing Lorne's footsteps, and they widened dramatically when he saw Lorne. He had obviously thought it was a nurse.

"Sorry," he mumbled and went to get up, but Lorne stopped him with a hand on his shoulder. "Jonathan? It's I that is so very sorry—"

"For what?" he shrugged. "You can't help how you feel."

"No, but I should have known better. I should have known that it wasn't true."

"What wasn't true?" Jonathan seemed to be choosing his words carefully.

"Dr. Coulson told me that you were taking the research job together. That you were getting married, and that we were moving, and that it was only because of Nana you broke your engagement in the first place. She stressed *we* because obviously now you had children you would need an omega to look after them. It would also be convenient as Nana would be in a separate apartment off the main house, so I could help her if needed. I would be well compensated and not to worry as I would be offered a nice retirement home after fifteen years."

Jonathan gaped. Then he narrowed his eyes. "And how did you find out it wasn't true?"

"Because Sophie and Suzanna gave me the presents containing the adoption certificates."

Jonathan leaned back closing his eyes and dropped a gentle kiss on Nicky's head before he stood up and carefully arranged him back in the incubator. He brushed a gentle finger over Nicky's cheek before he looked back at Lorne with what seemed to be complete disinterest.

Lorne's heart hammered in his chest. Had he been wrong? He eyed Jonathan. Watched the longing glance, he gave to the other two and then understanding dawned. He still wasn't demonstrating any trust. It was easy to change your mind with irrevocable proof. Lorne still had to prove he could make a leap of faith.

"It wasn't all your fault," Jonathan said. Lorne looked into his deep gray eyes. They seemed even darker, but maybe it was because they were full of hurt.

"You took me on faith," Lorne whispered and took a step closer, gratified when Jonathan didn't take a step back. "You took me on trust from the second I came to the clinic." He winced. "No, from the second you offered me shelter. And all I have done is question and doubt you at every turn. Believe others that have been less kind, less generous. Less...*everything*. And I have no idea why."

A small smile played on Jonathan's lips. "If I had talked to you—"

"When?" Lorne asked softly. "When I was in surgery? When every day we were fighting to keep them alive?"

"Jonathan?"

They both glanced back, and Dr. Coulson was there with a puzzled look on her face, glancing between them both.

Lorne ignored her because she didn't matter. He smiled at Jonathan and held out the papers he had brought. "These just need signing."

Jonathan didn't return his smile or look down. Fury was etched on his features as he stared at Anne. "Get out."

Anne's worried look turned shocked. *"Jonathan?"*

"You *lied*. You manipulated Lorne, not caring how much your dishonestly would hurt simply because you wanted a certain *job*." He almost spat the last word.

She took a step toward him, and Lorne, unable to keep his feet still, moved protectively to stand in front of Jonathan. She sneered. "What exactly do you think you are doing? You would have lived in comfort for a very long time. It is the best an omega can ever hope for, and you should count yourself extremely lucky."

"No," Jonathan stepped up flush with Lorne's back and laid his hands on his shoulders. "I'm the lucky one."

Her lip curled in disgust and temper. "Really? Wait till the authorities hear about your attempts to interfere in omega contracts and rights. How you're involved in sedition and want to change the law. I promise you will be lucky to get a job cleaning hospital floors by the time I am through."

"He won't need to clean any floors." A quiet voice said behind them, and they all turned to see Professor Denholm standing there looking mildly amused. "He won't need to clean them because you will have already been on your knees removing every speck of dirt." He smiled at Lorne and Jonathan then focused on Dr. Coulson. "You are fired without references, except everyone who is anyone in the medical community knows you have been working with me and will want to know why you are no longer. Good luck explaining that."

She blanched, looked from one to the other without saying a word, then turned and nearly tripped hurrying to get out of the unit.

The silence was interspersed with the sound of monitors quietly doing their jobs.

Gregory smiled at them both. "I want an invite to the naming ceremony." He nodded at the babies and walked back out. Lorne was stunned. What had just happened?

Jonathan calmly turned Lorne around so they were facing each other. "That was why I said it wasn't just your fault. Why I should have got my head out of my ass earlier and questioned what she was saying."

"You have a nice ass," Lorne said randomly and put his arms around Jonathan's waist, needing grounding. Needing to know he wasn't asleep and having the best dream. If he was, he never wanted to wake up. He felt the answering rumble go through Jonathan then he stepped back and dug into his pocket for the sheet of paper he had with him.

"This is the standard mating contract for fifteen years between you and me. I already tore up the adoption papers."

Jonathan frowned and made no attempt to take it. "But why would you do this? This gives you no legal right over the babies. I could terminate your contract when they were fifteen and ask you to leave."

"Yes," Lorne agreed and breathed out a gusty sigh and snuggled against Jonathan's chest. "You could. But I trust you enough to know that you won't."

Another second and Lorne smiled. He'd felt the lips that gently pressed against his hair, and the arms that tightened around him. "You mean that?" Jonathan whispered, his voice cracking.

Lorne lifted his arms and wound them around Jonathan's neck. "Promise."

And Jonathan's smile widened. "Just so you know, I don't want fifteen years," he murmured just before he bent his head to seal their lips together.

"I want forever."

EPILOGUE

SEVEN WEEKS LATER

LORNE'S HEART was so full he honestly thought it was going to burst. Rowley had been pronounced fit and able to come home, so his brother and sister, who had been home for a few weeks, welcomed him into their nursery. They were finally a family.

And somewhere in all the crazy, the building work had been done. Nana had her own downstairs room. The library that had seen better days had been converted just for her, although she'd insisted on keeping all the shelves. She'd even had the carpenters put up a special low shelf that little fingers could reach, and the large sunny corner near the bay window now had three extra small chairs. Even though it was a little early, Nana insisted that's where they would read stories every day.

Of that, Lorne had no doubt.

Nana was a gem. She had helped with first Hope, then Nicky, as well going every day to see Rowley. Held the babies and comforted Lorne every night when he could only bring two home.

He had felt like he was abandoning Rowley, but Jonathan had cut back on his hours at the clinic, and they had all managed.

Nicholas was even thinking of relocating here. And between him and Jonathan, they had even chosen the site for the free omega clinic. Donations had been pouring in, and they were hoping to start building as early as next spring.

Jonathan had been as driven about the clinic as he was everything else, and he had been stunned when Lorne had suggested it be named The Kayden Elliot Omega Clinic. At least, Lorne assumed he was happy. He had been kissed breathless in front of everyone then thoroughly spoiled when they went to bed. He knew Nicholas had been trying to find Shay, but his alpha had moved, and it was proving difficult.

The bath was still his favorite place in the whole house. Although, he now had fond memories of the shower, the dressing table, the back of the bathroom door, and the alcove near the nursery. They were steadily working their way around the upstairs.

Much later, when the babies were all fed and asleep—they had maybe three hours before it would start again—Lorne snuggled up to Jonathan and burrowed into his side. "Are you happy?"

Jonathan kissed his cheek softly then nibbled along his jaw until he reached his lips and hummed in appreciation. "Mmm." He pretended to consider. "I'm not sure. I may need some more convincing."

And just as Lorne was wondering how to go about doing that, they both heard an indignant wail from the baby monitor.

Lorne snickered as Jonathan groaned and got out of bed, holding his hand out for Lorne. "Come on, Daddy, your family needs you."

And they always would.

Broken Circle

Eternal Circle

The Promise

The Dilemma

The Beginning

Full Circle

*some titles may contain MPREG

Innocents

The Innocent Auction

The Innocent Betrayal

ABOUT VICTORIA SUE

Victoria Sue fell in love with love stories as a child when she would hide away with her mom's library books and dream of the dashing hero coming to rescue her from math homework. She never mastered math but never stopped loving her heroes and decided to give them the happy ever afters they fight so hard for.

She loves reading and writing about gorgeous boys loving each other the best—and creating a family for them to adore. Thrilled to hear from her readers, she can be found most days lurking on Facebook where she doesn't need factor 1000 sun-cream to hide her freckles.

www.victoriasue.com
Sign up for the newsletter: bit.ly/VictoriaSueNewsletter
Facebook reader group: Victoria Sue's Crew

Made in the USA
Columbia, SC
02 February 2019